Waterlust

Waterlust

by Tamar Judith Rivers

Second Edition

For information regarding permission, write to Paul Kevin Smith, 7801 Shoal Creek Blvd, Ste 228, Austin, TX 78757.

Printed and distributed by
CreateSpace: an Amazon Company
www.createspace.com

ISBN-13: 978-1523617302
ISBN-10: 1523617306

Dedication

This book is dedicated to my parents, Jean and Joseph Stern, for their inspiration and unselfish love and support. Recently, my father told me he "kvelt" (Yiddish for "felt pride") when I wrote songs at the age of six. I hope he and my mother continue to feel pride in my wandering passage through life.

Tamar Judith Rivers, 1994

Editor's Preface

I first met Tamar Rivers in 1994 when I enrolled in a yoga teacher training program at the former Yoga House in Austin, Texas. When I went to take classes there, I would often encounter Tamar sweeping up leaves in the front courtyard. She had enrolled in the teacher training program the year before, and was diligently doing her work-study hours at the studio. We soon became friends. I found Tamar to be open and loving, quirky and interesting.

Tamar was dedicated to environmental and human rights causes. She worked at the Ecology Action recycling center, and often participated in rallies and demonstrations for peace and justice issues.

Tamar had been badly injured in a car accident in Mexico many years before we met; she had acquired hepatitis C through a blood transfusion at the time. She lived with the infection for many years, and unfortunately was not able to tolerate the side effects of interferon treatment for the virus.

Prior to her death from liver cancer in February of 2013, Tamar named me Executor of her Estate. One of the requests in her will was to publish her novel. Prior to the posthumous discovery of her will, I had not even known that Tamar had written a novel.

When I started reading Waterlust, I was captivated by Tamar's story of a woman working in the all-male environment of a shrimping boat in 1977. After talking with some of Tamar's other friends about the story, I got the impression that it is autobiographical.

I wish to thank my sister Amy Smith Valentine and my husband Dino Costa for reading the novel closely and offering many suggestions to improve inconsistencies in the grammar, word usage, and sentence flow. I am also indebted to the members of my book club, Daniel Brookshire, John Henrickson, and Kathleen Strong, who read the book and discussed their suggestions for improvements in our meetings.

I want to thank Tamar's friends Kathy Goodwin and Zo Lewis Patterson, and the lawyer for her Estate, Patricia Kelly, for their support during my work as Executor.

I hope that many people will now be able to enjoy this fascinating tale of a woman at sea, both literally and figuratively.

Paul Kevin Smith
Austin, Texas
October 2015

Acknowledgements

I wish to thank the numerous people who have read the manuscript and made suggestions, including my women writer's group. I'd especially like to thank Pat Littledog, Wendy Nine, Dave Schroeder, Takako Taylor, and my editor Chuck Taylor for suggestions, proofreading, support, and encouragement.

Tamar Judith Rivers, 1994

"A ship in harbor is safe, but that is not what ships are built for."

– John A. Shedd

Chapter 1

I was intoxicated by water, and my intoxication had led me to this harbor. The harbor was a kaleidoscope of colors and shapes, a semicircle of water fringed with boats, processing plants and beer joints. Nearly all the boats were shrimpers, easily distinguished by their two tall masts. Some were newly painted; others the gray of weathered wood, shabby and comfortable as old shoes. The scene hummed with activity, shimmered in the bright Texas light.

The air I breathed was warm and moist with an early morning promise of heat to come. Mixed with the smell of the sea itself was the smell of commerce – a mingling of oil and shrimp.

My work boots pounded the planks as I made my way around the harbor, stopping at each boat to ask if they needed a header. Shrimp boats have no deckhands. Instead they have "headers", whose primary job is to pinch the heads off the shrimp that are caught. I called out to groups of men working on the decks, and to lone inhabitants sitting idly inside the wheelhouses or galleys of their boats. I asked already-experienced fourteen-year-olds and grizzled old men. I spoke with drawling Texas rednecks and with soft-spoken Tejanos. On some crews these two groups mixed, but mostly each group kept to themselves. Occasionally I stopped at a boat where a woman in shorts and a halter top – probably the captain's wife – worked alongside the men. If a boat looked dangerously rundown, I passed it by without asking for work.

I detoured around a fenced processing plant, and then inquired at a boat from Tampa. The skipper, an old black man with a pipe clamped between his teeth, sat on deck in a faded lawn chair. He removed the pipe to speak, "I'd like to take you on my crew, but my boat's goin' into dry dock today – it needs a little work. Come back in four, five days, an' I'll take you." His eyes crinkling in the glare, he continued, "I sure would like to have a woman on this boat."

"Why?"

"A woman brings good luck."

That was a twist. Most of these men thought having a woman on board was bad luck. A woman could never be simply another crew member, but would always have some special effect for better or worse – probably worse.

Leaving the Tampa skipper on his disabled boat, I continued on my rounds, reflecting on the difficulty of my position. I was out of my depth here, a woman in a man's domain. I saw or imagined this in the expressions on every face: "You don't belong here." It took real courage to walk this dock, to hide the part of me that was scared, to assume instead a strong, confident extra skin along with my jeans, T-shirt, and cap. The shrimpers who didn't reject me lavished more attention on me than they would have given a man looking for work. Either way, I stood out as an oddity.

Yet I felt I belonged here – felt a strong pull towards the sea and the seafaring life. I was determined to find work on one of these boats, no matter how long it took.

The sun blazed like an active volcano in the sky overhead as I reached the end of the dock and then turned back, dispirited. Inside my car the steering wheel was almost too hot to handle; I gripped it gingerly as I headed towards the town of Aransas Pass and the beach beyond.

A giant pink cutout of a shrimp graced the entrance to town. "Aransas Pass – Shrimp Capital of the World" announced the lettering underneath. More shrimp boats docked here than anyplace else in the world, or so I'd been told. Driving on past the sign, I glanced at the ugly, squat buildings scattered haphazardly along the town's main street. A few minutes later the road opened up. Flat coastal scrub gave way to small channels of water. A larger channel between the mainland and Mustang Island could only be crossed by ferry.

During the ferry crossing, I got out of my car and leaned against the side rail. A sharp sea-odor drifted up from the water. Jellyfish hung suspended just below the water's surface like floating white balloons. A pair of dolphins leapt out of the channel and curved back into it, one slightly behind the other. Their motions mirrored those of the waves, their smooth arcs meeting little resistance. The ferry reached the island, and I slipped back inside my car and drove off the ramp.

The island, long, narrow and perfectly flat, hugged the mainland shore like a child seeking security from its mother. Clusters of beach shops lined the main road of its only town, Port Aransas. Down a side street, the beach road wound past sand dunes crisscrossed by tire tracks and sparse patches of sea oats. The salty tanginess of the air increased, and I arrived at the beach.

This beach was totally unlike the Pacific beaches I remembered from my childhood. No cliffs loomed in the background; there was no pounding surf, no icy waters to dip into quickly. Instead there was a long, flat expanse of sand, backed by dunes, extending all the way down the Gulf side of the island. The water was gentle and warm, the waves calm. Baked in shimmering heat for months, the sand was sometimes too hot to stand on. Crabs skittered in and out of the sea. When caught in nets by crabbers, they waved their claws desperately.

The sea was filled with life. From the particles of water themselves, dancing and glinting in the sunlight, to the myriad animals and plants nurtured in its vastness, the presence of life here was strong. I immersed myself in the turquoise warmth, spent hours swimming and jumping through the waves.

This beach on Mustang Island became my temporary home. There must have been wild mustangs here once, but civilization had chased them away long ago – a civilization now represented by vacationing families crowding the beach. At night I felt safer when surrounded by people. After one attempt at sleeping on the beach, getting lots of sand blown in my face during the windy night, I retreated to my car and slept on the back seat – with my legs sticking out the open door.

The next morning, a Saturday, the harbor was almost deserted. I made the rounds of the few shrimping boats quickly, and then drove back to the beach. Monday would be the Fourth of July, and I decided it would be a waste of time to look for work again before Tuesday.

It was a long, lonely weekend for me. I was far from home, wherever home was; actually I no longer had a home. Although surrounded by groups of people, I knew no one there; I had no one to call family or friend. I spent the time doing nothing but waiting – waiting until I could find work on a boat.

Monday, I decided to enjoy the day for its own sake. I found a quiet, unspoiled beach farther down the island and spend the day there. The beauty of the place touched me; I felt peace and confidence flow into me with the waves that lapped my body.

At dawn Tuesday, I swam briefly, showered, and then headed for the harbor. Unlike Saturday, there was a normal day's compliment of boats around the harbor's inner ring. I walked beside the boats, pausing at each to ask for work.

"Hey . . . do you need a header?" I asked at one trim-looking shrimper near where I'd started my search.

A sandy–haired man looked up at me from the deck. "Ever work on a boat before?" he asked.

"Yeah, on a tugboat."

"Ever been out in the Gulf?"

"No," I admitted.

He reached up to scratch his scalp. "This boat might need a header. Come back later when the crew's here."

I made a mental note of the boat's name, *Sea Rider*, then continued on. I was glad I had worked on the tugboat. While a lot of the particulars of the work were different, and we had been in coastal and river waters rather than on the Gulf, at least I didn't feel like an absolute beginner in this world of boats.

As I continued around the harbor, meeting indifference and disapproving stares, I daydreamed about my life on the tugboat, thinking about all the new skills I had picked up there. True, I'd done the cooking and mopped the floors, but I'd also learned to jump from dock to deck, scramble up and down ladders, throw ropes, and tie knots to secure the boat in channels where the water rose or fell. I had gone places and done things that women rarely do.

I continued around the harbor with only half my mind on the process of looking for work. I'd almost reached the end of the line of boats when a white sedan stopped on the road behind me. The driver called out to me, jolting me out of my reveries. I walked to the car and peered in the open window.

"I seen you lookin' for work before," he said. "We can prob'ly use a header on our boat. Get in, I'm goin' over there."

I climbed in and stole glances at the driver as we headed towards his boat. He had swarthy skin, prominent facial features, enormous eyes, and a great mane of dark, curly hair which fell to his shoulders.

"I'm Andres," he offered. He accented the second syllable and pronounced the final "s" with a Spanish lilt.

"My name's Ruth. Are you the captain?"

"I'm the rigman."

A rigman is second-in-command on a trawler. He's responsible for the nets: hauling them up and down, and keeping them in good repair.

The boat Andres took me to was the *Sea Rider*. She was a fair-sized shrimper, maybe sixty or seventy feet long from bow to stern. Painted white with dark green trim, she appeared seaworthy and well-cared-for.

Gradually I realized that the sandy-haired man was the owner. He looked up at Andres and said, "You should have a good catch this time; the radio says they're really jumping."

"I think so," Andres replied. "We take two headers this time; we make sure we can handle it."

The owner frowned. "D'ya think this boy'll make it? He's never been in the Gulf before . . . I hope he don't get seasick."

"I'm not a boy," I protested. But the owner seemed not to hear me, so I let it go by.

"He be fine," was the rigman's deadpan assertion.

I realized the owner had encouraged me earlier because he thought I was a man. Occasionally boat people had asked me whether I was a man or a woman. With my short hair, small breasts, and work clothes, some of them were unable to tell the difference. Andres knew I was a woman, but was willing to humor the boss.

"Come on," Andres beckoned to me, "we go do the shopping."

As we drove through town, he pointed out the house where Preacher, the captain, lived.

"I think Preacher's sleepin' late," he said. "We all went drinkin' last night . . . Preacher, he's my cousin."

We drove to the local supermarket; with Andres directing, we filled cart after cart with foodstuffs for the voyage. The bill came to just over four hundred dollars, and Andres paid with some sort of voucher. When we returned to the boat with the supplies, the owner was standing on the back deck with another man.

Andres nodded in the newcomer's direction. "That's Preacher, the captain."

Preacher had short hair slicked back from his face and small, regular features. While not very tall, his open shirt revealed an unusually broad chest. He reminded me of a bull.

Right now he was on the back deck with the owner looking at what appeared to be a wooden door, but was actually a component of the net, used to weigh it down so that it would drag the bottom.

The owner was grumbling, "Goddamned carpenters make a fortune these days. Cost me eighty dollars to get this fixed!"

In Spanish, Andres murmured, "If I had his money, I wouldn't complain about eighty dollars."

Preacher smirked, "Correcto."

The owner complained, "I wish you guys wouldn't talk in Spanish all the time; I can't understand you." Shortly thereafter he left.

Andres tilted his head in my direction, telling Preacher, "This is the new header."

The captain looked at me. "The work's pretty rough out there right now; do you think you can handle it?" Unlike Andres, he spoke English precisely.

I shrugged and said, "No work, no money."

I was expecting the captain to decide whether I had the job or not, but apparently everything was settled. The men went off to find another header.

I was brimming with barely-suppressed excitement: finally I was going out on the open water. While I brought my gear on board, I thought back on how I had first come to this area. . . .

I'd been living in Santa Fe for about two years when my friend Holly asked me to travel to Texas and New Orleans with her. My life had settled into a monotony of petty details. I had stayed too long in one place, and I was ready for a change.

The country we passed through was new and exciting for both of us – the long string of bright lights and looming mountains of El Paso in the dark, the seemingly endless stretch of desert ending in a series of monumental mesas to the east, then on into the green and gently rolling Hill Country of Central Texas. From San Antonio we left the main highway to explore the back roads; we wound our way south towards Corpus Christi.

We never did get there. We picked up two hitchhikers who were going shrimping, and decided to check it out ourselves. From what they told us, the money was fantastic. But I was less interested in the money than I was intrigued by the adventure and the chance to be out on the water. After two years of the arid Southwest, I was ready for water – ready for large expanses of it.

We spent the night in Aransas Pass, sleeping on the floor at the home of a shrimper the hitchhikers knew. The next morning Holly and I drove early to the harbor to look for work. May is early in the season, and there was not a lot of activity. Late in the day we gave up and headed for New Orleans. But a seed had been planted in my mind, and I was determined to find work on a boat, to live on the water for a while.

Everything about water attracted me. I loved the sound of it, from the high rushing sound of brook water over stones, to the roaring of ocean waves. I loved the slippery, caressing feel of water, the clean smell of fresh water, and the strong smell of salty brine. I aimed to surround myself with water.

Now I was back in Aransas Pass again, with a job on a shrimper which was due to leave the harbor in just a few hours. When I got back to the boat, Andres was on the back deck with the other header, introduced to me as Frog. A tall, slim Chicano in his late teens, he had an unfocused expression and a complexion scarred by acne.

I realized that we hadn't discussed my pay, and figured we'd better get that settled before we left. I found Preacher in the wheelhouse and asked him about it.

His eyebrows shot up. "You'd better ask Andres."

I found Andres coiling a rope on the back deck and asked him. Without looking up he said, "First, I'll see how you work."

"That's no good," I cried, my face flushing with anger. "Tell me what you're paying me now, or I'm getting off." The boat was about to leave the dock at any minute.

The rigman looked up at me. "Do you think you're worth ten dollars a box?"

I felt my anger subsiding. "That's fine."

A box is a hundred pounds of shrimp. Headers are paid a certain amount for each box of shrimp in the total catch. From having asked around the harbor, I knew that ten dollars a box was generous for an inexperienced header. Eight dollars was more usual. The rigman got a higher figure per box, around eighteen dollars, and the captain got a percentage of the total catch. Everything depended on how the shrimp were running. The pay for a two-week voyage could vary astronomically. A header could make sixty dollars or a thousand, or more likely, some amount in between. I liked this method of payment better than getting a salary. It meant we all shared in whatever luck the boat might have, good or bad, and it was to everyone's advantage to see that the work got done.

Andres asked me to sit on a raised wooden platform in the middle of the deck, the hold cover, so I'd be "safe and out of the way" while he and Frog prepared the boat for departure. I watched the procedures, feeling bewildered and useless. I was intensely excited about the voyage, and also a little apprehensive. I really knew nothing about these men, and I had very little idea what would happen when we were out in the Gulf.

Chapter 2

After the rigman untied the boat from the pier, I moved to the side rail to watch our departure. I felt I was moving backwards as first the harbor, then the shore, slipped out of view. We passed through the sheltered waters close to the coast, and then glided beyond the barrier islands, moving out into the open sea. Turning my back on the dim outline of land, I watched our forward progress. The salty air had a crisp feel and tangy smell. The horizon became immense; broad plains of sea and sky surrounded us on every side.

Water is a strange substance: slippery and hard to grasp, present in large masses yet breaking into tiny droplets, rocked by the moon's pull into constant motion. Its motion was barely perceptible in the harbor, gentle in the land-sheltered waters, and increased to a vigorous rolling and pitching beyond land's sight.

Once I had taken a Guatemalan boy to see the ocean for the first time. I watched as he ran excitedly around the beach, his eyes very bright, experiencing the crash and roar, the froth and salty spray, as wave upon endless wave hurled itself against the barrier of land.

This gigantic power, which never ceases in its movements, is unlike anything else on earth. It cannot be adequately described through words or pictures, but must be experienced.

As I looked at the sea, I tried to imagine how I would describe this marvel to someone who had never seen it. I thought of a field of wheat: rippling, shimmering, alive in the wind. But there are infinitely greater variations and nuances of movement in the ocean. Unlike wheat, the sea is translucent, reflecting the colors surrounding it. I gazed at the water, noticing the clear blue surface, with hints of green on the near side of each ripple. I caught glimpses of the obscure depths below.

Andres leaned on the rail beside me. "You feel OK?" he asked, doubtfully.

"Uh-huh, I feel fine."

Minutes later, the unaccustomed motion got to me. I churned up my lunch, spewing it over the railing. Right away my stomach felt calmer, but it took only a few minutes for the whole cycle to begin again. I had taken some seasickness medicine before we left the dock, but it had had no effect. I vomited again five minutes later and then, trembling and sweating, I groped my way to my bunk. Lying down felt better. I found if I stayed horizontal, I only had to get up and vomit every few hours, whereas if I tried to sit up or walk around, I got sick continuously. Gone was my infatuation with the sea; my entire consciousness was contained in my convulsing stomach, spinning head, and shaky, sweat-covered limbs.

Soon there was no solid matter left in my stomach; I started having dry heaves. Each time that happened, I got up and drank some water and swallowed a few crackers so I'd have something to throw up. The water on board tasted vile; I had to force myself to swallow it. Of course I wished the boat would turn around and take me back to port, but I was not quite ready to give up.

As I was sitting in the kitchen, grim-faced, stuffing crackers in my mouth, Andres came in and said, "I bet you wish you was in your casa right now."

In spite of how desperately sick I felt, he enabled me to see the humor in the situation. "You know it!" I agreed.

"You should have thought twice about going shrimping."

Well, I should have thought three times, but it was too late for that. I would've given anything just to be on solid ground again, ground that didn't roll and pitch. I felt that I would never get over this seasickness – that it would bring my shrimping career to a brief, inglorious end.

Andres was the only one who would talk to me. "Eat a lot and walk around," he advised; I was unable to do either.

He was sympathetic, but refused to take care of me. If I asked for something, he would say, "Go and get it."

"I know this sounds crazy," Andres began, "but sometimes if you clear out one end of your body, the other end'll feel better. You want to try some Ex-Lax?"

I nodded my agreement. But within minutes I was heaving the chocolatey stuff into the toilet bowl. So much for that experiment.

The hours passed by in a blur between sleeping, waking, and vomiting. Day faded to night, and I was vaguely aware of the crew tromping out to the back deck, and then in again, saying that the catch was good. Mostly I slept. I couldn't even imagine working.

Once during the night, as I sat exhausted at the galley table, Preacher sat down opposite me. "You know," he said, "I'm taking a big chance having a greenhorn like you on my boat." I said nothing. His remark struck me like a punch in the gut. Still, I was grateful he said "greenhorn" instead of "woman."

Sometime in the morning, Andres walked into the bunkroom. "Hey, are you still in bed?" he asked cheerfully. "Come out on the back deck – I'll show ya somethin'."

Unsteadily, I followed him outside. The salt spray and fresh air were a welcome change from my stuffy bunk. Another shrimp boat was anchored behind the *Sea Rider*, back-to-back. Two dark men stood on the deck looking at us.

Andres explained, "The one with the sunglasses, that's Shades, Preacher's brother; he's a captain, too. The other one's Pablito, his header. Pablito, he's sick like you are."

I shouted, "Are you seasick?"

"Naw," Pablito yelled back, shaking his head vehemently, "hung over." Maybe he was seasick, but he'd never admit to it.

"I wish we had some Dramamine for you," Andres said to me.

"I have some."

"Híjole, girl, why you don't take it?"

"It didn't help yesterday, but I'll try it."

This time the Dramamine worked. I showered, washing layers of rank sweat off my body, and then changed into clean clothes. I was still a little shaky from the boat's pitching, but the nausea was gone. I was getting my sea legs.

While I was sick, I had barely noticed my surroundings. Now I took the time to look around. The back deck, our working area, was the only large exterior space. Two large spools, wound with thick metal cable for supporting the nets, were located near the front of this deck. Just in back of them was the hold cover, five feet square, raised off the deck about eighteen inches. A portion of this cover could be lifted off, revealing steps down to the area where the cleaned shrimp were packed in ice. Behind the hold cover was a large open space with the apparatus used to raise and lower the nets – ropes, pulleys, and tackles. The deck was surrounded by a three-foot-high railing, which extended all the way around the boat. The side decks were mere walkways enclosed by this railing. The front deck was small and roughly triangular-shaped, coming to a point at the bow. The anchor was located there, along with a smaller hold cover which led to the engine room.

The interior of the boat was compact. Overlooking the back deck were two small bunkrooms. These were identical except that one room and its bunks faced the bow, while the other room sat sideways to it. Since the wave motion was bow-to-stern, this gave the crew the choice of being tossed head-to-heels or side-to-side as we slept. My bunk was the head-to-heels type.

In front of the bunkrooms was the galley, the largest interior space on the boat. This room contained a small sink, stove, and refrigerator, as well as a booth-type table for meals. It was a walk-through room, with doors leading to every other room and to the deck. One side door led to a small bathroom, so small in fact that the whole room became a shower stall when anyone took a shower. Forward of the galley was the wheelhouse, a semi-circular room with many windows where navigation took place.

This space was to be my home for the next few weeks. No longer sick, I was ready to participate in the work and the life of the boat. It was a strange life, and a strange schedule, by land standards. The nets were mended, and then set out to drag early in the evening. Several hours later we pulled them up and headed the catch by the illumination of floodlights on deck. The process was repeated three times during the night, and we ended up heading the third catch as the sun was rising. We ate breakfast, and then slept until mid-afternoon, when the cycle began all over again.

On this day before dinner we all went out to the back deck to set out the nets. I sat on the hold cover to watch and learn. Setting out or pulling up the nets was a long, involved procedure, and at first I had only a general idea of what was being done.

Shrimp boats have two tall masts rising from the back deck. They are raised up in port, but out in the open water the masts are spread out horizontally to the sides with nets attached, so that the boat appears to have wings. The nets are raised and lowered off the masts with ropes and metal cables. The nets are roughly conical in shape, and contain baffles, so that whatever sweeps into them is trapped. The boat travels for several hours while they're filling. Small nets called "try nets" are brought up first. When the catch in these looks good, the larger nets are hauled up, and their contents dumped onto the deck. Right away they're lowered again so that they drag the bottom for more shrimp while the crew is heading the first catch. With push boards connected to long handles, the catch is swept into one large pile, and the crew sits down on low stools to sort through it and head the shrimp. Shrimp's heads must be discarded so that the shrimp will keep during a two- or three-week-long voyage. Hence the title "header."

Andres showed me how the heading is done. He crouched on a low stool facing the catch pile, and using a small scraper, raked a portion of the catch in front of him. Wearing rubber gloves, he flipped through this assortment of sea creatures, picking up several shrimp in each hand. Holding the base of the shrimp's head between thumb and forefinger, he snapped his fingers together so that the head fell off, while the shrimp's body remained in his palm. The snapping is done with both hands simultaneously so that two shrimp are headed at a time. After both the shrimp in his hands had been headed, he opened his hands over a tub at his side, and the shrimp fell into it.

After watching Andres, I tried it. At first I was pretty slow. Andres kept an eye on my work for a while, and then said, "I make a deal with you. You cook and keep the inside of the boat real clean, an' you don't have to do none of the outside work."

"But I just started doing this. Give me a chance – I'll get the hang of it." I hadn't come out on this boat to be relegated to women's work.

"OK," Andres agreed, "I see how you do."

Standing up after an hour or two on one of those low stools was no easy matter. At first my back felt like it would never return to a fully upright position, but the worst stiffness went away almost at once.

Andres and Frog opened small gates in the railing at deck level, grabbed the push brooms, and started sweeping all the junk fish off the boat. I was not expected to help, so I staggered inside, numb and exhausted, and sat in the wheelhouse. Preacher was in the captain's chair, watching the progress of the boat through the large windows. Occasionally, he walked over to the instrument panel and made an adjustment in the course set on the automatic pilot.

Soon the rest of the crew came in. Everyone sat down, half asleep, waiting to pick up the nets and clean the second catch of the night. We had very little time to wait. After Andres checked the try nets, we all stumbled out to the back deck. While the captain helped bring up the nets, the boat ran by itself – an unsafe but widespread practice on shrimpers.

Soon the nets were dangling over the deck. Not only did they contain our catch, but also several beer cans and a large, rusty barrel. Grimly Andres worked to untangle the barrel from our net so that we could empty the catch out onto the deck.

With the nets emptied, we sat down to head again. Andres was unbelievably fast, Frog came second, and I was slowest. I was pushing myself hard to gain speed, and just to make it through the night. The air was thickly hot and humid, with a faint sea breeze. Day or night, there was no escape from the heat, which pressed in on us, and I wondered if that was why we did our shrimping at night.

A whole new world of sea creatures – mariscos – was revealed to me, creatures caught and hauled up in our nets. A pungent smell permeated the air, as a mound of undulating flesh covered the deck like a giant amoeba. It was mostly gray, but with patches of brown, dull red, and delicate blue. Soon separate creatures begin to emerge. Crabs scurried across the deck. Fish thrashed about, shrimp squirmed. Eels slithered. Creatures of all sizes and shapes, all fighting hopelessly to find the sea once again, without whose nurturing waters they would soon die.

The shrimp, flounder, and red snapper would be sold for food; the deaths of the others served no purpose. I wished there was a way to exclude them from the catch or sweep them back overboard before they died. But all our attention went to sorting out and heading the shrimp as fast as we could. With three of us working, this still took several hours. By that time what remained on deck was a lifeless mass – garbage to be swept overboard.

The sun rose as we headed the third catch, and Andres unfurled awnings overhead to shade us as we worked. This time Preacher came out back and helped. He threw the shrimp he headed in with mine so that my pile grew faster. Occasionally he walked over to the side rail and peered around front to watch for other craft.

Once as he was heading he looked up suddenly and raced to the wheelhouse. Then I felt the boat change direction. He walked back and said, very matter-of-factly, "We almost crashed with another boat. I had a feeling I should get up there, and was just in time."

No one said anything; we continued heading as fast as ever. This incident had an unreal quality for me. Nothing up front could be seen from the back deck, and anything I couldn't see at the moment didn't quite seem to exist for me.

The heading completed, Andres sent me inside to cook breakfast while he and Frog cleaned the deck and iced down the catch. I mixed up a batch of biscuits, and then set a pot of coffee on to perk. I made the brew deliberately weaker than had been my habit in New Orleans. I fried up some sausages, then eggs, tilting two onto each plate as carefully as I could. With the grease sliding around in the pan, and the floor rocking under me, it was not easy to cook. Several of the yolks broke and I saved them for my own breakfast. Although I was too exhausted to have any appetite, I felt I should eat something. The long hard night was coming to an end, and soon I would be able to sleep.

Over breakfast, Preacher said to me, "I'm very proud of you. Not many greenhorns could last all night, but you did."

I practically glowed. I had never worked that hard, never pushed my limits before. I was sure the praise was genuine – until I had proved myself as a worker, Preacher had practically ignored me. I was ready to knock myself out doing any kind of work for this man.

Chapter 3

At dawn the anchor was lowered and everyone went to get some much-needed sleep. Andres and I shared one bunkroom, Preacher and Frog the other. These rooms were pared down to the minimum of furnishings, to maximize the utilization of space. Each consisted of two narrow bunks, one on top of the other, a strip of floor just wide enough to stand on, and a wooden locker with an upper and lower compartment. Frog and I, being the lowly headers, were relegated to the windowless lower bunks.

Except for the lack of windows at the lower bunk level, these rooms felt good. Given the wide-open expanse surrounding us on every side, this measured, orderly space was a comfort. The only annoyance was the heat. A small fan was provided for each bunk. By keeping the fan on high, and the door and windows open, there was just enough air circulation so that sleep was possible.

This boat was much smaller than the tugboat, where I had had my own room. There was no privacy here, and I slept in shorts and a tank top. The men slept in their underwear, bare-chested, and stood beside their bunks to throw on their clothes. Soon Preacher suggested that I do the same, in order to keep cool. "No one will bother you," he added, and I accepted his suggestion. Besides being cooler, it simplified changing clothes. Before I had closeted myself in the bathroom to change; now I just stood by my bunk and threw on whatever I was going to wear. Boots and work pants were kept outside, so that their fishy stink didn't invade the living space.

We all woke in the late afternoon. Religiously I took my Dramamine, fearful of another bout of seasickness. Andres handed me a package of meat, already defrosted.

"This is stew meat," he said. "You think you know how to fix it?"

"Sure."

He walked out to the back deck. Frog pulled up anchor, and then went to help Andres repair and set out the nets. Preacher kept watch. I coated the chunks of meat with flour and browned them in a large pan. As the meat began to sizzle, a rich aroma filled the room. Then I added chopped vegetables and water, turned down the flame, and covered the pot. With the stew simmering, I went out and leaned on the railing, watching the sunset and singing to myself:

Every evening when the sun goes down,
I hang my head, oh Lord, in mournful sound.

I like pensive songs. There was no one to hear, no walls to contain the sound, and I let my voice soar over the endless waves. Several shrimp boats were visible clustered together to the west, darkening to silhouettes. Past them I could see a huge oil tanker; with its smooth windowless bulk it resembled a floating fortress. I slipped inside and joined the captain in the wheelhouse.

A singsong voice in an unknown language was piping on the radio.

"What's that?" I asked.

"Ain't you ever heard that before? That's Cajun French."

"Oh. Sounds weird."

"A little while ago," said Preacher, "some of these Texan boys were on the CB radio, cussing out us Mexicans and calling us dumb 'cause we were talking in Spanish and they couldn't understand us. So I got on the radio, and said, 'You're the ones that're dumb, 'cause we can speak two languages, an' you can only speak one.'"

"Absolutely," I agreed, "It's just sour grapes."

"When I grew up, things weren't like they are now. There was a lot more prejudice against us Mexicans. An' you couldn't complain 'bout discrimination – that didn't cut no ice back then."

The room was quiet. I looked around the wheelhouse. It was the nicest room on the boat. The walls formed a semicircle with the curved part all windows from chest level on up. Glass doors on either end completed the rounded portion and opened onto the narrow side decks. Below the windows were a large spoked wheel and the navigation aides: radar, CB radio, a depth-sounding gauge, and the automatic pilot. The back wall was wood paneled and split in half by the door from the galley. On one side sat the captain's chair; on the other, two rows of benches with cushions. This was where I was sitting – on the top row so that I could see out more easily.

As we sat in this room, the motion of the surrounding sea was rocking us constantly. The water was darkening along with the sky, but I could still make out the waves. I fixed my gaze on one patch of sea, and watched as the water swelled to roundness, then flattened, only to be immediately followed by a new swell. I felt how the forces of planetary pull were constantly at work. I imagined the whole sea as an immense pot of boiling water, continually bubbling up.

Preacher broke into my reveries. "I used to have a girlfriend that worked on boats, a tugboat Annie." he smiled wryly. "She was alright; damn if she wasn't a strong little thing. Is this the first time you worked on a boat?"

"No, I worked on a tugboat just before I got this job – out of New Orleans. I got the job by calling just about every marine towing company in the New Orleans yellow pages. But it was worth it; it was beautiful. We went up this incredible river in Alabama, up into the Cumberland Plateau. There was nothing along that river – it was like traveling through a jungle."

"Sounds like a pleasure trip."

"It was in a way. There wasn't much work to do. There were two other deckhands. We were supposed to be scraping and painting, but there were only two scrapers, and every time I started using one, the captain would come out and ask me was the work getting too hot or too heavy for me."

We laughed together over this. "I think the captain preferred to see me in the kitchen. I don't mind cooking, but I wanted to do other things, too. He did let me tie the boat up in the locks. I loved doing that, especially getting to stand up there on the barge, ahead of the boat and away from everything, while the boat plowed upriver. I felt so free out there, like I was floating or flying."

I thought about the captain of the tugboat – how he had always been trying to control everyone, how he kept pestering me to sleep with him. That part of the trip hadn't been so free. Then, at the end of the trip he'd congratulated me for not getting involved with anyone on the boat.

Preacher asked, "What made you come out here on the water with three crazy Mexicans?"

"I like the water. Besides, I needed a job."

"You ever been married?"

"No. You?"

"Yesss," he drew out the sound. "This is my third marriage, and I'm supporting all of my wives. The kids too – I got a bunch of little Indians. Like they say, 'If you wanna play, you gotta pay.'"

"Damn . . . What about your present wife; are you gonna stay married to her?"

"I'm thinking about getting a divorce and remarrying my second wife. See, my present wife and I don't have much in common anymore. When I married Linda I was a Pentecostal; I was born again. She's in the Church. She don't like my friends; she won't drink; she won't go out and party. Besides, she's too young for me; she's only eighteen; I'm thirty-six. How old are you?"

"Twenty-seven. Did you put that sign up in the galley when you were a Pentecostal?" The sign overlooked the table and read "GOD BLESS OUR HOME" in mock embroidery.

"Yup," said Preacher, "I was into Jesus for quite a while there. I actually was a preacher for a while; that's where I got my nickname. But I stopped believing. After that I felt like a hypocrite, so I quit preaching and I quit the Church."

I reflected on this. "I haven't been religious since I was a kid. Once when I was in fifth grade, I doubted God, and then I accidentally stapled my finger. I thought God had punished me as a penance for my sin. By the year after that I'd stopped believing in God altogether."

The rest of the crew came in and began talking together in Spanish. Andres was speaking rapidly and laughing, his face flushed with excitement.

"Don't think we're talking about you or want to leave you out," said Preacher, "it's just that we always talk in Spanish."

"It's your language. I know some Spanish – Mexican Spanish – but I can't understand the way that you all talk."

"We talk Tejano Spanish," explained Frog.

Preacher asked me, "What nationality are you; you're kinda dark, like us."

"I'm Jewish."

"Oh," said Preacher, "a Christ killer!"

I laughed – he was obviously not serious. We joked around a while longer, and then I moved to the galley to season the stew and fix a salad.

At dinner I ate very little; that way I wouldn't feel queasy.

"You going to fly away, you keep eating like a bird," Andres warned me.

He carried the kitchen garbage out to the side rail and heaved it overboard. I was reminded of the beer cans and the rusty barrel which had come up in our nets the previous night. I hated seeing the Gulf mucked up, but we really had no choice unless the owner was willing to buy a garbage compactor. He would never spend the money unless it were required by law.

I washed the dishes, and then joined everyone in the wheelhouse to watch TV until it was time to pull up the nets. I felt happy there. I was being treated as a fellow worker, a comrade. It seemed like some kind of invisible bond was forming between me and the crew.

Since I would usually sit on the hold cover while the nets were being pulled up, I had time to observe the crew working. I loved watching Andres and Preacher. Their ways of moving were totally different, yet each seemed just right. Both had been shrimping on and off since their mid-teens; their movements formed a graceful unity with the work they were doing. They hauled the nets up in a state of concentrated awareness, which probably approached meditation.

Andres was totally fluid, scrambling lightly from one part of the deck to another; effortlessly throwing his body behind the ropes he pulled and the levers he held. He had the sinuous grace of a large cat – a mountain lion perhaps.

Preacher, in contrast, was deliberate and grounded, moving at the ropes like a karate practitioner going through a *kata*. At some point he must have analyzed all the motions involved in his part of the work. He performed them slowly and thoroughly, although he could move quickly if necessary.

Frog, at nineteen, had none of the grace and sureness of the other two. I had no idea what kind of figure I cut on deck. After once catching me standing with my hands in my pockets, Andres told me to take my hands out and keep them out, for as long as I was on deck. I never forgot that, and the advice has had a lasting psychological effect on me – making my hands and body more ready for action.

That night one of the wooden tackles hit Andres across the back of his hand, and his hand swelled up. "My hand hurts a lot, lots, but I still work," he bragged. I had some knowledge of massage, and tried rubbing it for him, but it did no good. Andres said, "I used to know a gypsy woman. If she rub your hand, all the swelling go away. When we dock in Galveston, I'm gonna go to the Marine hospital. If you work on a boat, it don't cost nothin' to go there, don't matter what you need."

Galveston was the shrimpers' party town. We planned to go there on a weekend sometime before the voyage was over. The crew talked about getting loaded there, maybe picking up women. I looked forward to Galveston as a change from the everyday routine of the boat, as a new place to explore, and as a chance to walk on solid ground again.

As we headed the shrimp, Andres pointed out to me some creatures to avoid. There were eels whose bite is poisonous, and a goldfish-sized fish edged with red which could inject a poison that would cause temporary paralysis. Now and then as I was heading, a crab tried to crawl up my leg. Absorbed in my work and caught unawares, I would jump. This amused Andres to no end. "It won't hurt you nothin'", he said. "Why you jump?"

This night I was not quite as exhausted by the work. I helped sweep the junk fish off the deck after the heading was finished, then stayed out on deck to watch the rest of the process. First Andres washed the shrimp in a chemical solution, which acted as a preservative. Then he lifted the cover off the hold and climbed down the steps. Frog handed down the baskets of shrimp; Andres spread them out in thin layers and shoveled ice over each layer. When he finished, we all went inside.

Preacher was standing in the wheelhouse, putting a tape in the cassette player. The tapes on the boat were mostly rock and country – many by groups from Texas. One song I found peculiar:

> If you're down and confused,
> And you don't know which way to turn,
> Go find a Mexican whore,
> And take all your troubles to her.
> They all call her Puta,
> But nobody knows her name.
> Her Mama was a whore,
> And her Daddy was the Ace of Spades.

Well, maybe she had troubles of her own, but nobody seemed to consider that.

There was silence for a while, then Andres asked Preacher, "Are you really gonna divorce Linda?"

"I reckon so," Preacher answered.

Andres said, "I wish I'd a never married Consuelo; she got gripey after that."

"Was she that way before you got married?" I asked.

"Naw, just afterwards."

"Well maybe it's from being cooped up with the kids all the time," I suggested.

"Naw, it's just the way she is."

"You like being married, man," Preacher put in, "That way you can get some anytime you want."

"I know," Andres agreed, "I can't get used to being out here without any. I'm gonna find me a bitch in Galveston. You won't see me around here till the next morning."

Tiring of this tough-guy banter, I slipped outside and leaned my elbows on the smooth wood railing. The moon was full or nearly so, making the night particularly beautiful. Like magic powder, silvery-white light spread over the water's surface, accenting the peaks and caps formed by the constant shifting of the waves. Pinpoints of light indicated other crafts, each a self-contained universe. I felt fortunate to be surrounded by so much beauty.

I reflected on the fact that so many aspects of the water element have traditionally been considered feminine: the sea itself, from whose nurturing waters life first appeared; the watercraft, which ply her expanses; and the storms and hurricanes, which threaten sailors.

If the sea, ships, and storms are thought of as feminine, I suspect it is because sailors so miss the feminine in their lives that they endow their surroundings with female attributes. Perhaps also because the sea, and the storms which churn up her depths, are powerful, mysterious, and frightening – all attributes which men see, or imagine, in women.

In the morning Shades' boat was again anchored behind the *Sea Rider*, and Shades swung across the connecting rope hand over hand – no easy feat – to have breakfast with us. He had a guitar slung across his chest, which he lent to his brother Preacher. Shades was taller and slimmer than Preacher. His eyes were invariably covered with sunglasses; his expression was one of constant amusement. A stubby beard covered his square jaw, and a pipe was always clamped between his teeth. After breakfast the two of us sat at the galley table and talked.

"What made you want to do this man's work, Boy?" Shades asked me, his smooth voice gliding over the words. Shades' nickname for me was "Boy" – I suppose to accentuate the fact that I was a woman doing what he considered to be man's work.

"Curiosity," I answered him. "I wanted to see what it was like, and to see how well I could handle the work, not just do the cooking."

"Well I'm glad you do cook. It sure is good to eat some home cookin' for a change. Don't nobody cook on my boat."

"No? You're the captain – why don't you order one of your crew to cook?"

"Oh, I'm like my brother. Neither of us likes to give orders, to make a big deal outta bein' the skipper. Some captains wear them skipper hats – you've seen 'em – them black hats with the visor in front. I think they're stupid, myself. An' some of 'em won't let none of the crew sit in the wheelhouse – wheelhouse is out of bounds. Naw, I don't like to play captain."

"Then I guess you don't get no grub. What's your boat like?"

"It's small, nowhere near as nice as this one. The owner don' wanna put no money into it. He's a cheap bastard . . . a rich man's always cheap."

"Have you been married as many times as your brother?"

He laughed. "Naw, just once, and I'm still married to her. I got me a buncha little Indians, too. You ever been married?"

"Nope."

"Preacher tol' me you're a Christ-killer," said Shades, kind of grinning around the pipe in his mouth.

"You don't know how many times I heard that growing up. Kids I didn't even know would come up to me in the yard at school and say, 'My Daddy said you killed Jesus.' I'd get so angry and scared I'd be shaking."

"I hear what you're sayin'," Shades responded, "I don't think about it too often, but growing up Mexican here in Texas was pretty rough."

"I bet it was."

"Us minorities ought to stick together . . . How about you and me gettin' married?" he asked, and we both laughed.

"You know, Boy," Shades said soberly, "you lucky to be on this boat. These boys treat you real good."

"Oh, I know it. I'm happy to be on this boat."

"You're crazy in the same way all of us is crazy, so it work out good . . . I gotta get back to my boat. I see you later, Boy."

After he left, I fell asleep in my bunk, and dreamed. . . .

Chapter 4

Narrow Victorian houses lined the pavement. Janine and I walked hand in hand up a hill like a roller coaster until we reached our house. Night was falling, and we spread a quilt on the backyard grass, stripped off our clothes, and lay down in each other's arms. Body against body, we were melting, fusing, floating on a cloud of feelings.

I awoke and found myself not in San Francisco, but on a Gulf shrimper. I was surprised and pleased to have had such a beautiful dream about Janine, a lover from years ago. The strongest part of the dream was the feeling of floating, and this feeling lingered with me. It was strange – floating was literally what we did on the boat all the time, but it didn't always feel this euphoric. I felt like sharing the dream with someone, but realized that would be a mistake.

I had started waking up before anyone else in the afternoons. It was the only time I could be alone, and, as long as I took my Dramamine, I was well enough adjusted to the ship's motion to read and write letters.

The next to wake up that day was Andres. He sat down in the galley opposite me, rubbing his injured hand, which looked even more swollen than it had the night before. "What are you looking so pleased about?" he asked.

"I had a beautiful dream. I dreamed I was . . . making love." Almost before the last words were out of my mouth, I bitterly regretted having said them.

Andres rolled his eyes. Emphatically he said, "Oh, you dreamed you was makin' love!"

The moment marked a new phase of my life on board. Andres started teasing me constantly, asking when can he "have some" and feeling me up. A few times he told me that he had also had a dream about "makin' love."

At supper, I asked Andres to sharpen the kitchen knives for me.

"Sharpen them on your ass," he replied.

I said nothing.

"Why don't you answer him?" asked Preacher.

"Because I don't know what to say."

"Tell him to sharpen them on his own ass; it's rougher. Fight fire with fire," the captain continued, "If Andres feels you up, shove your fingers up his ass. That'll stop him."

I was grateful to Preacher for the advice, particularly since he didn't have to get involved. Quickly I learned how to exchange insults with Andres, how to fight fire with fire. I tried to take it all lightly, or at least to give that appearance – one of the worst sins in the code of honor for these men was to take yourself too seriously. Up to a point, dishing out insults that were as good or better than those received was fun and sharpened my wits. But being constantly harassed, and constantly throwing back the same, was a tiring process, and I wondered where it would lead in the end. I longed for the early days on the boat when Andres had treated me as a co-worker and a comrade. True, he had given me some extra help and attention because I was a woman, but it had been an innocent sort of attention.

Life on board was becoming more complicated, and I found I had unexpected feelings to deal with. Living in such close contact with men, and with men that I liked, I was becoming increasingly sexually aroused. My body seemed to be on fire; I had never felt quite that way before. Partly, I relished the feeling. I had been told by previous male lovers that I wasn't a "real woman" because I didn't become aroused easily. While I had tried to resist the message, part of me had soaked it up. I had always longed to be easily turned on, even constantly turned on – now I had my wish. Clearly I was reacting like a "real woman," and it was good for my self-image. Besides, I liked the intense, tingly feeling in my body.

But being easily turned on had its own problems. I knew that it was best, in terms of my relationships with the men on board, not to sleep with any of them. But my sexual feelings were intense, and I didn't know if I could wait for gratification until the voyage was over.

I considered the fact that both Andres and Preacher were married, but I didn't feel guilty or disloyal to their wives. I knew the men slept around anyway. I felt, perhaps rationalized, that the boat world is another universe from the land world. What happens on a boat doesn't count in the real world. However, I doubted that their wives felt the same.

The wives weren't my problem – the boat was. I knew that sleeping with any one of these men would damage my working relationship with him, and with all of them, really. And I wanted to keep working on the boat.

There were miserable aspects to this life – the odd hours, the monotonous work, feeling dirty and sweaty all the time. Showers were rationed – one every three days – so that our water supply would last and we could stay offshore longer. But for me the positive aspects far outweighed the negative.

Despite my disagreements with Andres, I felt intensely alive there. I liked the camaraderie, the feeling of being part of a family on the boat. I enjoyed having my strength and endurance challenged, and I loved being surrounded by the unending sea and sky.

The elements here were powerful, and I never tired of watching the surface of the sea arching and straightening in endless lithe movements, like a crystal ball before its depths cleared.

Sweeping my eyes over the vast horizon I felt not like a tiny isolated creature, but like a part of the sky I surveyed. I observed, but was also a component of these changes, these cycles of the day: the transitions from light to dark, with all the varying shades of color and intensity in between. The sun, moon, and stars; the wind and rain; the sunrise and sunset which I partook of every day as if it was for the first time in my life; all this richness touched me more intimately than it had since my childhood, when all the world had been new. The world was new to me again.

I also loved the tiny space of the boat. It felt like an anchor in the vastness, but it was no place for keeping secrets. If I slept with one of the crew, I wanted no one else to know about it; I didn't want to be shared around. Undoubtedly, the men were feeling the same tension I was – I thought it best to leave things as they were. I began pleasuring myself in my bunk, learning how to do so in total silence. This helped a little, but only just a little.

Despite his teasing and other faults, I was most attracted to the rigman, Andres. I admired the easy, graceful way he used his body. He had enormous energy and magnetism – something which had always attracted me. Reason told me not to act on that attraction, but I am by nature impetuous; really the only thing keeping me from jumping in the bunk with Andres was that I had no birth control. I hadn't packed contraceptive foam when I had gotten the job, because I had been determined not to sleep with anyone on the boat, and especially not to be forced to. I decided to buy some foam when we docked in Galveston.

I was sitting in the wheelhouse with Preacher, who was playing "Tom Dooley" in a rudimentary fashion on the guitar, while also keeping the watch. With a final chorus of, "Poor boy, you're bound to die," Preacher set the guitar down, and we sat in silence.

"Was there ever a woman on the crew before?" I asked.

"Yeah, there were some, but they never wanted to do no work. They just lay around in the bunks bein' sex objects."

"Really?" I was surprised. I wondered if this account was less than objective.

"But those women had a choice. Once, I was on a boat where the captain kept this woman as a sexual slave, an' there was nothin' I could do 'cause I wasn't the captain."

"Jesus. I don't see how you could watch that and not stop it."

Preacher shook his head. "There's gotta be order on a boat. A boat is just like a country – someone's gotta be in charge. Now you take Jimmy Carter. I don't agree with him, but I support 'im 'cause he's President; he's the one in charge."

I disagreed. "That's what's wrong with this country – too much blind obedience. People need to think for themselves and do what they think is right."

"Nope," Preacher said firmly, "The captain's the law on a boat, 'n' that's the way it's gotta be." A sly smile crossed his face. "Wait 'til I tell Andres we got a mutiny on our hands."

He picked up his guitar and strummed for a while, then returned to the subject of female crewmembers.

"You know," he mused, "I was pretty doubtful about taking you with us. I said to Andres, 'Are you sure you want to take what's-her-name?' I didn't think you would work out. But you're a pretty good worker. Now if the owner had known you were a woman, we wouldn't have been allowed to take you. It's really none of his business, but that's his rule."

"He thought I was a guy, and when I said I was a woman he didn't hear me, so I let it go by."

"It's much harder havin' a woman on the boat. You have to treat her as a fellow worker – you can't just say, 'Drop your drawers.'"

"Andres does," I pointed out.

"Well Andres is somethin' else. Besides, he would never hurt you – none of us would. But Andres is out of

54

line sometimes. I had to get on his case a few times for gettin' out of hand with his old lady."

"I like Andres – he can be real sweet, and helpful too. But when he's in a bad mood, he takes it out on Frog and me, and that's not right."

"A person should always have control over their feelings," said Preacher. "I try to be fair to everyone around me, no matter how I'm feeling about them. Take Frog," he chuckled, "he's a funny kid – kinda scattered. He's not careful with the ropes, doesn't know what he's doin' – 'n' that's dangerous. But I don't bear him no ill feelings."

Gradually, Preacher and I were becoming friends. He was by far the most interesting person to talk to on the boat.

In contrast, Andres' conversations consisted of short, high energy bursts, mostly about sex. "I used ta read a lot of books," he told me once.

"Oh yeah?" I asked, surprised, "What kind of books?"

"Porno books." And he broke up in laughter.

Our youngest crewmember, Frog, was quiet and shy. When he talked, it was about his family, or his dream to buy a boat one day. Andres treated him deplorably, but Frog never complained. Andres called him "African nigger" – on account of his dark complexion, and was always finding extra work for him to do. I pointed out to Andres that there's nothing insulting about being black.

Replied Andres, "I don't think you like it if I call you African."

I shrugged. "I wouldn't mind."

"No? We had a nigger workin' on the boat once. He'd get seasick – like you. But he kep' workin' anyway . . . I got some nigger friends at home."

I gave up. Like some other Southerners I've met, Andres used "nigger" as a put down, yet seemed to have nothing against blacks as people.

But clearly he had a grudge against Frog. One day instead of dropping anchor, Andres ordered Frog to keep watch while the rest of us slept.

"Why don't you just drop anchor?" I asked.

Andres eyed me belligerently. "You think you know how to run the boat?"

"No, but I just don't see why Frog should have to keep watch all day."

"When you can run the boat, you take over my job."

Frog was forced to work around the clock with hardly any sleep. Preacher's attitude towards whatever Andres did was that "you an' Frog are Andres' hired hands." He didn't interfere, although he claimed to be fair to everyone.

Another time Andres confided to me, "We gotta get Frog off the boat before he kills us all. He don't keep his mind on his work. But not you – we want you to stay." While I felt sorry for Frog, I was pleased that Andres and Preacher wanted me on the boat.

What Andres said about Frog was true – he made mistakes, and mistakes made on deck can kill. There was constant danger on the boat – of being slammed in the head with a tackle, swept overboard, going down in a storm, or colliding with another boat. Anyone not doing the job competently increased the danger. Once I asked why no one wore hard hats on deck. "We gotta whole closet full," Preacher replied. "You can wear one if you want, but them hard hats ain't hard enough to help you if one of them tackles hits you on the head."

It still seemed to me that wearing a hard hat was a good idea. But, not wanting to look ridiculous and wanting to be "one of the guys," I also went without one. I never worried about danger while I was on the boat. I had confidence in Preacher's and Andres' knowledge and ability to pull the boat through. More importantly, I accepted the presence of danger as part of the deal and left it at that.

About 5 a.m. one morning the crew hauled up the nets from the third drag of the night. In the process, a cog on the winch broke. Andres and Preacher managed to get the nets up anyway, but there was no way to do more fishing until the winch was welded.

"Looks like a trip to Galveston," Preacher commented dryly.

We had breakfast as usual, and then settled down to sleep. Lying in my bunk that morning, drifting between waking and sleeping, I had a curious vision. I saw human embryos floating in a sea of fluid. Each embryo had both female and male sex organs; each had a penis tucked inside its own vagina, forming a yin/yang, a male and female creature which was complete in itself. I saw the embryos growing older. As they grew, one organ withered away and the other developed, so that each became either female or male. Each craved sexual union as a return to the original, blissful state of wholeness experienced in the womb . . . loving was coming home to wholeness.

Waking more fully, I contemplated my fantasy. Undoubtedly it was influenced by my present state of incredible sexual arousal. There was nothing I wanted so much as a man inside me, his body in close contact with mine, forever.

Still, I found the fantasy interesting for its own sake and, although not literally true, I felt there was a great deal of truth to it on a fanciful, symbolic level. This vision seemed not to encompass love between two people of the same sex, but I felt that it actually did in some way that was beyond my understanding.

I joined Preacher in the wheelhouse and described the fantasy to him. He listened gravely. "There's some truth in that," he commented. Barefoot, in shorts and a T-shirt chopped off above the navel, Preacher stood squarely behind the wheel with its polished wood spokes as he steered towards the Port of Galveston. Wearing an identical outfit – Preacher had cut one of my T-shirts for me so I would be cooler – I sat cross-legged in the captain's chair and regarded the Gulf.

Sunlight flashed on the water's surface and brilliant beams of light danced on the ship's wheel. Suddenly I saw this wheel as the Wheel of Fortune of the Tarot deck, and we in the wheelhouse were characters of the Tarot. Preacher was the Charioteer, confidently directing the course of the boat; Andres was the Magician, applying himself to the many different tasks in the ship, controlling everything with ease. Frog was the Fool, following an unknown path with a dream in his pocket. I was the High Priestess, enthroned in splendor. We were charting a path through the sea of all possibilities.

The captain switched on a tape, jolting my mind back from all possibilities to the present one. The song was "Lucille" by Kenny Rogers.

"Country songs never tell the woman's side of the story," I complained.

"Aw, they're just a bunch of male chauvinists," Preacher replied.

Delighted with his reply, I said, "There's only one advantage to being a woman in this country that I can see, and that's not having to go in the Army . . . Were you ever drafted?"

"Yup. The Army was my downfall. Before I was drafted, I was the cleanest-livin' kid you ever saw." Preacher shook his head sadly. "A few weeks in boot camp changed all that. My folks almost didn't recognize me; I was drinkin' beer, smokin', and cussin' up a storm. Then I got sent to Vietnam.

"Were you wounded there?"

"Only a broken heart." He looked at me suspiciously. "You weren't one of them anti-war demonstrators, were you?"

"Yeah," I admitted, "I was in jail once for a couple of days."

"Ha," Preacher snorted, "that's no reason to go to jail. I been in jail a few times – once for bootlegging. The other time I prefer not to talk about. But I don' believe in that protesting stuff. A country has to have discipline – just like a boat. Everybody can't be pullin' in different directions."

"Everybody is pulling in different directions, anyway," I pointed out. "Most everyone's just out for themselves."

Preacher shrugged, pulling out a navigation chart and studying it. The chart was covered with tiny black triangles.

"What are those?" I asked, pointing to one.

"Those are snags – places to avoid."

"Damn, they're all over the place. I don't see how you can read these things."

He shrugged his shoulders. "Just practice is all."

"I've been wondering . . . how come we shrimp at night?"

"Them brown shrimp dig into the mud during the day; mostly they only come out at night. I don't know why, but once in a while they'll be really jumpin'. When they're like that we keep puttin' the nets out during the day and they still come up full of shrimp. But most times they'll dig in during the day an' you can't find any."

"Well," I said, "I'm glad they're like that, because it sure is cooler to work at night. I'll talk to you later, I gotta start supper."

I moved my fan into the galley, then seasoned a plateful of flour and started breading pork chops. Andres came up to me, stood close behind me with his hands on my hips, and asked, "When you gonna give me some?"

I laughed, moving away from him. "Never . . . When you hired me, did you think I was gonna sleep with you?"

"Damn right. Why else would I hire you?"

"I'm a good worker."

"You a cold bitch." Andres sat down at the table with a girlie magazine and started flipping through it. "I like to be rich for a week so I can have me a lot of bitches." He showed me a picture of a voluptuous blonde. "My ambition is to sleep with a blonde like this one," he informed me.

"Do you ever want to sleep with someone because of how you feel about them, not how they look?" I asked.

"My daddy said never turn nothin' down."

"Well, just because your daddy said it doesn't mean you gotta do it."

"Oh, I do it; I never turn nothin' down."

I continued breading pork chops and laying them in the frying pan to brown. Andres continued flipping through his magazine, and then said, "I don' really want to be rich. If you rich, you all the time got to be worryin' about someone takin' what you got. I think if I stay poor I have a better life. But I just wanna be rich for a week so I can have me a lot of bitches."

He started rubbing his injured hand. I had forgotten about it. "How's your hand?" I asked.

"It still hurts – lots. I think maybe somethin' is broken."

"Better have it looked at in Galveston."

Preacher called us both into the wheelhouse and pointed out his brother's boat, the *Miss B*, cutting in front of us.

"Shades is courtin' you, Ruthie," said Preacher, laughing. "He wants to marry you."

"He's already married."

"He gonna have two wives," said Andres.

Shades circled us several times, then glided off into the distance. We all laughed at his outrageous nonsense.

After dinner, around 10 p.m., Andres ordered Frog and me to wash the inside walls of the boat. At first I thought he was joking, but no, the boat needed to be "shipshape" before we docked. The pork chops had made me feel queasy, and shortly after I started on the walls I had to visit the john and dispose of my dinner. This was the first time I had been sick since my marathon bout of seasickness; I vowed to avoid greasy food for the rest of my time on the boat.

Frog shared cleaning the inside of the boat with me, and the deck cleaning with Andres. The *Sea Rider* was kept quite clean, like every boat in which its crew takes pride.

When I moved into the wheelhouse to clean the walls there, the rigman followed me in. "Stay away from the wheel," he cautioned, "if it start to move and you're cleaning back there, it break your arm."

There was no heading to be done that night, and once we finished the walls, Frog and I were allowed the luxury of sleeping till morning.

Chapter 5

By daylight we were approaching the Port of Galveston. We had been at sea only five days – but land was suddenly fascinating to me, and I was unable to take my eyes off the shore. At first it was only a dim shadow, but as we moved closer the shore loomed larger and more distinct. The land was low-lying and densely covered with vegetation. Finally we moved into the harbor itself, and were surrounded by other watercraft of every sort: tugboats with their tall stacks, motorboats, oil tankers, ocean liners, and lots of other shrimpers.

We settled into a space and Andres tied the *Sea Rider* to the dock. It was Sunday, so the cog couldn't be welded until the next morning; we had the whole day off. Andres pulled out some hamburger patties to thaw. "You don't have to cook today," he told me, "We all fix our own supper."

The first thing I did was take a long shower. We would be picking up more water before we left, so I was able to use as much as I wanted. Then I stuffed my mucked-up work clothes into a duffel bag and set out to find a laundromat. Meanwhile, Preacher and Andres drove off with a waterfront buddy to buy dress shoes for the evening's adventures. Sunday is a bad day for partying, but they intended to do their best. I found a drugstore near the laundromat, with the goal of buying some contraceptive foam. The drugstore was closed – I would have to buy it in the morning.

Every time I had been seasick I had longed to be on solid ground again. Now I found that my body had to readjust to land; I saw and felt motion where there was none. As soon as I stood or sat in one place, the scene around me began to sway rhythmically, making me dizzy. I used to feel sorry for boat crewmembers who had to stay on board overnight when they were in port. But now I realized that once you're used to the water, it's much more comfortable to stay on your boat, which rocks gently even in the harbor. Walking, I soon discovered, was much better than standing still. And so I set out to explore the street fronting the harbor.

The street curved away from the harbor and I passed faded wooden houses where dark women sat on porches enduring the heat. Wistfully they seemed to wait for something to happen – I doubted that it ever would. I passed bars blaring pop tunes. Outside, groups of patient, dusky men gathered. Clad in faded overalls, they also seemed to be waiting for something to happen. Suddenly the neighborhood changed and I was walking through the fashionable part of the waterfront. Old buildings, restored and painted bright colors, housed antique shops and restaurants, one of which I turned into and drank some cider to cool off amid the dusty heat.

Then I headed back towards the boat, watching the same scene unroll backwards. Frog was the only one on board when I returned. He was sitting in the wheelhouse listening to music. I decided to take advantage of the semi-privacy to masturbate. I closed the door (it had never been closed before), turned on the fan, and, under cover of the top sheet, removed all my clothes. I spread lotion on my breasts and caressed them, first holding them in my hands and squeezing gently, then brushing my fingertips over my nipples so that they stiffened. With one hand enclosing my breast, I slowly slid my other hand down. There was a knock at the door. "What is it?" I asked, annoyed.

"You left this shirt in the wheelhouse."

I extended one arm from under the sheet, opened the door a few inches, and took the shirt. Then I resumed where I had left off, although the mood had been somewhat spoiled. Several minutes later there was another knock.

"Yeah?"

"It's lonely out here," Frog complained. "Why doncha come out and keep me company?"

I sighed. It seemed that Frog couldn't handle being alone. Regretfully I pulled on my clothes and joined him in the wheelhouse. We listened to the cassette player and talked.

"I sure was glad to get this job," Frog said. "My family, they need the money. This trip – we gonna make out all right – but nothin' fantastic. One trip I made a thousand dollars in two weeks. There was lotsa shrimp then – lotsa work, too. I was headin' shrimp till my fingers was bleedin'!"

"Musta been a lot of shrimp, to make that much money . . . I don't know if I could work like that," I mused. "Maybe, maybe not."

"Some women is strong. I seen this chick truck driver – she was built like a wrestler. She hadda unload these big, heavy boxes from her truck, so I went over there to help her. She look at me, an' say, 'What you doin' over here, boy?' So I say, 'I come to help you unload.' Well, she look at me an' she say, 'I don't need no help.' So I left."

I laughed appreciatively. Then we were quiet for a while, listening to the music. I wanted to be alone – wanted to write letters – but I knew Frog would keep pestering me. I doubted there was a library near the waterfront, and it was too hot to sit outside and write.

"My family lived in Colorado for a while," Frog said wistfully. "It was real pretty there – I liked it a lot. But there's better money here, in shrimping. I wanna save a lotta money, someday buy me a boat. They cost a lotta, lotta money; about two hundred thousand dollars."

"Jesus, that is a lot of money," I said. It seemed to me that Frog had better learn how to do his job before considering buying a boat. But he was still young; he might get it together eventually. I didn't think he would ever be able to buy a boat, though.

Presently Preacher and Andres returned. We had a casual meal of hamburgers, and then Andres asked me, "Why don' you come out to the bars with us, Ruthie?"

"Might as well," I said.

The three of us set out after supper. Frog stayed on board – he wanted to save his money. We walked along the harbor road, all of us dressed in clean jeans and T-shirts. The men had on their new dress shoes; I wore sandals. I felt neither female nor male; I didn't know how to be with these men outside the confines of the boat. Preacher was distant towards me; I sensed that he didn't want me along. On the way to the bar, we stopped at a pay phone. Andres and I stood a short distance away while Preacher phoned a lady friend. Evidently she was not home, and we continued ambling along the harbor road. The bar we entered was semi-deserted. Andres and I ordered beer, Preacher whisky. Preacher paid.

We sat in silence until the captain looked at the rigman and said, "Let's go to a strip joint."

Quickly we finished our drinks. Having no desire to watch strippers, I walked back to the *Sea Rider* alone.

Andres and Preacher returned to the boat about 11 p.m., looking sheepish. Clearly, neither of them had gotten laid; they didn't even seem particularly drunk. "Wasn't nothing goin' on," said Andres, disgusted. "Sunday night."

When I woke up the next morning, welders were fixing the winch on deck, and Andres was off at the supermarket. Hastily, I threw on some clothes and told Preacher that I had to get something before we left. The drugstore was now open, and I bought a container of contraceptive foam. I didn't know if I would use it, but having it gave me the choice. Andres returned with beer and ice cream, but with none of the food staples we needed. His hand was still swollen; although we had been in port twenty-four hours, he had never bothered to go to the medical clinic.

Chapter 6

Ropes were untied, the anchor was raised, and the *Sea Rider* was gliding through the carnival collection of boats in the harbor – all sizes, shapes, and colors of rigs, bright new ones and decrepit old ones. We passed out of the calm waters sheltered by the island into the immensity of sea and sky – sea and sky seemingly going on forever – the Gulf of Mexico.

Our masts were spread out once again – our wings above the water. Life on board returned to its everyday routine. I washed the breakfast dishes, mopped the floors, and then settled into Andres' bunk, where there was a breeze, to smoke and relax. After a while Andres walked up and stood by the bunk, his sleek body exuding a magnetic energy.

"Hey, Ruthie, kin I lay up there with you for a little while?"

"Sure." I moved over to make room on the narrow bunk. My body was tingly. I was ready for whatever happened next.

Andres wrapped himself around me and looked me squarely in the eyes. "Do you want to make it?" he asked.

"Yeah."

He bounced up on the bed and hastily removed his clothes. "OK, let's do nasties. Take off your clothes, hurry up."

Something in my mind jerked awake. This frantic rushing was not what I wanted. Andres was grabbing at my tits, jiggling my ass. "Your ass is like Jell-O," he said.

"Forget it," I said abruptly, "I changed my mind."

"OK," he replied, in a casual tone.

I was vastly relieved that Andres was taking this lightly. I tried to explain: "I can't just make it like that. I like to do a lot of touching, to get into it with someone." Andres was no longer listening. I felt he had lost interest.

I couldn't understand why someone would reduce making love to just plain fucking. Here was a man who was sensual in his every movement, yet when it came to performing in bed, all that sensuality vanished. I wondered whether his wife liked it like that. Or was he different with her? I'd like to know, but thought better of asking.

So we lay up in Andres' bunk, touching and talking. It felt good, this undemanding physical closeness, and it seemed to drain away some of my sexual frustration. Preacher walked by on the deck and saw us through the window. "Aaeeii!" he cried, and we laughed.

"You know," said Andres, "you can come up here and share my bunk anytime, anytime you want. I won't do you nothin'."

After a while I climbed down to my own bunk and slept. I woke before the others, sat out by the side rail, and contemplated the water. The simplicity of this life, and the grandeur of the surroundings, put me in touch with a level of awareness beyond the ordinary. I felt a kinship, a oneness, with all living things. I was overflowing with love for everyone on earth. I felt connected to the earth, the water, the sky; all sharing the same spark, all pieces of a larger whole. I was reminded of the Woody Guthrie song "Tom Joad", which describes everyone in the world as being part of one big soul.

I have had this feeling only a few times in my life. I wish I could have it all the time, but it soon escapes me.

Later, when Preacher was perched on the captain's chair, keeping watch, I told him about the experience.

He listened gravely. "There's got to be some sort of power," he commented. "I've felt something similar to that – it's the sea that does it. There's so much power here, every now and then you're able to see things in a different way."

"Do you think Andres and Frog have ever felt it?"

He thought a minute before replying. "Hard to say. If they did feel it, I doubt they would know how to talk about it."

That night we again shared in the work of the boat, finding and heading the shrimp, which paid for our voyage and our existence. This life and this work was simple and poetic, or boring and tedious, depending on one's point of view and length of time spent shrimping. These men had been shrimping since they were fourteen or so, and they all claimed to hate it. I thought partly they hated it, and partly they loved it. This life that was so much freer than working nine to five, so consciousness expanding, could also be incredibly confining. A boat can be a widening universe, the quintessence of freedom, or it can be a prison. It can even be both at once. Shrimpers stay with their trade because it's all they know, because there's money to be made, because they're hooked on the sea, or for some combination of those reasons.

The shrimp that came up in our nets that night were giants – larger than my open hand. Preacher picked one up. "White table shrimp," he proclaimed. "These're the best there is. Save some out and Ruthie can fry them up for supper tomorrow."

This was the first time we had eaten any seafood. I had often thought about putting aside some shrimp, fish, or crab for my own supper, but I had always been too exhausted to go to the extra trouble. I could eat seafood everyday, but the rest of the crew wanted their meat, so meat it generally was.

In the morning Andres cooked breakfast, claiming he was tired of my cooking. He fixed bologna and eggs. I barely tasted it; I hate bologna. "You better eat; you gonna waste away to nothin' at all," he warned me.

I watched the waves for a little while, and then climbed into the bunk with Andres like he had said I could. Already he was asleep. Still asleep, he got an enormous erection. Quickly, he pulled down my panties and was inside me. "Wait," I whispered, pulling my body away from his. "I have to do something." I climbed down to my bunk and filled my vagina with foam. How could I have been so stupid as to sleep with this man and not expect him to fuck me? I would rather have stayed in my bunk and forgotten the whole thing; but it seemed a lousy time to back out.

I climbed back into Andres' bunk, got on top of him, and pulled him inside me. He didn't move. Apparently my being on top was too much for him, so I allowed him to turn me over. Andres' eyes were closed, and he was pretty much still asleep, but he began to hump me frantically. Somehow it didn't feel that good having him in me – like someone scratching an itch with one finger when you want them to use their whole hand.

Frog walked by on deck and saw us, and I felt ashamed. Afterwards, we both jumped up and went to different ends of the boat – compelled by some sort of reverse magnetism.

When I woke up I headed to the kitchen galley, took some steaks out, and started chopping onions to prepare the meal.

"Hey Pan, is my lunch ready?" I stood still in shock, a faun surrounded by hunters. Literally "pan" means "bread," but it also means "cunt," and Andres had never called me that before. I didn't like it, but saying so would only make matters worse. The code these men lived by said not to take yourself too seriously. Much as I hated it, the word in Spanish didn't bother me the way it would have in English; it simply didn't carry the same load of associations. Just let anyone on the boat say "cunt," and I would quit in a minute.

Pan – cunt – I was determined never to be Andres' cunt again. He might have had me once, but he wouldn't have me again.

Andres was in a foul mood. He had had his chance to demonstrate his masculinity, his virility, and he had failed. Our sexual encounter didn't come out the way he had expected, the way either of us had expected. So he took his moodiness out on me and Frog, as he always did. There was no way to avoid him – the boat was too small, and I had to work with him on deck and share a bunkroom with him.

"Why did you come up to my bunk when I was asleep?" he hissed when no one else was within earshot.

I shrugged. After feeling so alone on the beach, I had wanted some warmth, some touching, and some affection. Instead I had gotten a hard fuck. With all my being I wished I hadn't climbed up into his bunk. Lord knows I wished I hadn't, but wishing will get you nowhere. I couldn't possibly say any of this to Andres, so I merely shrugged my shoulders miserably.

We ate our lunch and later, while I cleaned the dishes, I heard the crew in the wheelhouse talking with Shades in Spanish over the CB radio. I didn't understand the conversation, just occasional phrases. One phrase caught my attention, hit me in the chest like a physical blow. "Sus nalgas son buenas," flowed out of Andres' mouth, and they all laughed. Literally, "she has a nice ass," but I translated it at the time as, "she's a good lay." I was wound tight with shock and anger, but let on nothing.

The afternoon faded into evening. Andres was touchy, impossible to be around. I avoided him as much as I could, eating supper in the wheelhouse with Preacher, whose presence was restful.

After supper we tromped out to the back deck to haul up the nets and head the first batch of shrimp for the night. As we were heading the shrimp, Andres pointed to a rock crab. "You ever see anything as ugly as this?" he asked. The crab was dark-colored; warty bumps protruded from its shell as it went skittering about the deck. Andres raised the handle of his scraper and plunged it through the crusty shell. The animal waved its claws wildly while Andres struck it again and again. Its back smashed to bits, the crab ceased to move, ceased to live. Andres laughed wildly, then went back to heading the shrimp.

"Why'd you do that?" I asked.

"It was ugly. I kill it because it's ugly."

After the frenetic activity of the first haul, I sat in the wheelhouse with the captain. The night enveloped us in tranquility as we conversed. A country song wound around the tape heads in the cassette player, filling the room with music.

"I once lived with hillbillies," Preacher began lazily, "down in Alabama. Those were some of the best years of my life. I was bootleggin'. Those people were so good to me – they shared everything they had with me."

"We went up a river in Alabama on the tugboat. Sure is pretty country."

"Yup. I had me a woman there – a white woman." There was a tinge of pride in his voice when he said that the woman was white.

"What happened to her?" I asked.

"I left her because of her jealousy. I couldn't walk out the door without her pestering me about where I was going and when I was coming back. One day I couldn't take it anymore, and I just up and left. Ain't seen her since."

The tape stopped playing. Preacher got up and switched on another one. "I gotta wake Andres up. S'time to haul up the nets."

"It feels so peaceful in here," I said. "I don't even feel like going out there."

"Then don't. Stay here with me."

So I stayed a little longer and chatted with him. Andres came in after the work was done and yelled at me, but after he heard it was the captain's idea he shut up.

In the morning, to my surprise, I headed more shrimp than Frog. As it got light, Shades' boat, the *Miss B*, appeared behind us.

"We finish these shrimp an' have breakfast, then we gonna have us a party," Andres announced.

Shades came over to have breakfast with us. As usual, he was merry and mischievous. "When you gonna marry me, Boy?" he asked.

"You're already married," I pointed out.

"Don't matter; I'll have two wives."

I fantasized about switching boats and shacking up with him.

We rolled out awnings on the deck to shade us from the sun, and then carried out beer, watermelon, and ice cream for the party. Shades attached a rope ladder to the side, climbed down, and swam in the Gulf. I followed. This day the waters were calm, but it still required a lot of energy to swim there. Also, I had to keep an eye out for jellyfish. I have always loved the water. I would like to be a fish, a dolphin, or a mermaid. I want to swim with dolphins someday.

Exhausted, I climbed back on deck. The header from Shades' boat, Pablito, was there, as was Alex, another relative, also a captain.

"Why don't you wear a bikini?" Shades asked me.

"I don't have one." If I had one, I wouldn't have worn it there.

"She don' need a bikini," put in Preacher. "She's all the time wearin' them Daisy Mae shorts."

Everyone laughed. My shorts, the only ones I had, were cut extremely short and slit up the sides. The men all wore their cut-offs at a conservative mid-thigh length.

Shades looked my way. "So how's it goin', Boy?"

"I'm tired – I've been working hard."

"You mean to tell me," he began, incredulous, "that you call sittin' on one of those stools for a couple of hours hard work?"

I grinned. The way he described it, it didn't sound like work.

"Well," Shades continued, "are you gettin' to be a better header?"

I bubbled over with laughter. "I headed more shrimp than Frog today."

"It's true," said Preacher, "She did."

"You still takin' them seasick pills?"

"Naw, I stopped . . . I'm pretty used to the boat now."

"You know," said Shades, "when y'all docked in Galveston, I thought that would be the end of you. I never expected you to last in this mis'rable life."

"I'm still here," I answered dryly. The way things were going with Andres, I didn't know how much longer I would want to be on the boat, or would actually be on it.

Right now Andres was darting glances like daggers at me. He didn't like my spending so much time with Shades. I didn't care, but I expected him to take it out on me later.

Alex was also watching me. "Why don't you come work on my boat?" he offered.

"I like it here," I replied warily. I didn't trust his offer.

"Where's your rigman?" Alex asked Shades.

"He over there on my boat practicin' his guitar. He don' wanna 'sociate with us lowlifers – he too pure, too Christian."

Andres laughed. "It's his loss; we have a better party without him."

A joint was passed around. All the while, the boat gently rolled under us, as natural now as the apparent stillness of the land. Shades pointed out a grey funnel-shaped mass towering over the water a few miles away. "That there's a waterspout," he pronounced, and then asked, "Ain't you afraid?"

"No."

"Why not?"

"Because I know if there was anything to be afraid of, you all wouldn't just be sitting here on deck."

Shades chuckled. "You right. Waterspouts ain't nothin' to worry about."

The waterspout dissipated before reaching our boats.

"Hey, Boy, you wanna go steady?" Shades asked. "We could go to church together on Sundays in Aransas Pass."

I laughed. "I bet you're too hung over on Sunday mornings to go to church. Anyway, you'd never get me in a church."

"Why not?"

"I can't forgive the things they did to my people."

"You can't blame the whole religion for that," said Shades. "That's like saying because Pancho Villa was bad all Mexicans are bad."

"That's not the same thing, but I don't know how to explain it . . . Wanna go for another swim?"

"Let's go."

When we climbed back on deck a few minutes later, the party had wound down considerably. Exhaustion from the night's work was beginning to show, and soon the partygoers from the *Miss B* returned to their boat to sleep.

"I want to talk to you," said Andres that afternoon. "I don't want you tellin' nobody that we made it together."

I was flooded with relief. So he hadn't told anyone, didn't want anyone to know. What he said on the radio to Shades must have just meant, "She has a nice ass."

"I won't," I said, "but Frog saw us through the window."

"He won't say nothin' to nobody . . . What made you come up to my bunk, anyway?"

"I just wanted to sleep next to you, that's all."

"Well," said Andres, "that's what you get."

I grinned and the tension between us melted away – at least the extreme tension did. I thought Andres regarded me and liked me as a person, but when it came to sex, he thought of me, and of all women, just as objects, separate from any personal relationship.

The next time I walked into the bunkroom I saw that Andres had tacked a towel up over the window as a curtain. I smiled to myself. Curtains wouldn't make a difference. Whatever Andres thought, I knew I would never sleep with him again.

Chapter 7

That night the nets were hauled up covered with a gelatinous material – jellyfish. Frog and Andres had to work with them. The jellyfish stung them plenty; they raked their fingers over their arms and legs and shook them off. Preacher stood by my side, watching. "Ain't you glad you don't have to do that?" he asked.

I shrugged. "I would if I had to."

Between hauls I sat in the wheelhouse with the captain and the rigman. I asked if either of them had been to Mexico. They laughed and exchanged comments in Spanish. Then Andres said, in English, "Yeah, we been down there, but we can't understand how they talk."

"Really?" I knew a fair amount of Mexican Spanish, and already I was starting to pick up some of the crew's Tejano dialect. "The way you talk doesn't seem all that different to me."

"Oh, it's different," said Andres.

Preacher said, "When I go down there, they don' allow me to carry my gun, so I hire me a bodyguard. The girls down there call me captain." In a falsetto voice he mimicked them, "Mi capitán, mi capitán." He laughed and said something to Andres in Spanish. I imagined what big shots they must appear in Mexico. The money they earned would be a fortune by Mexican standards, and I was sure they were generous with it.

"Let's take the boat to Mexico," I suggested.

"The captain laughed, then shook his head. "Naw," he said, "we got work to do."

The next afternoon Andres walked up to me in the wheelhouse, looked me squarely in the face, and asked, "Do you want to be treated as a man or as a woman?"

"As a man," I responded. I had been on the boat long enough to understand what he meant. Being treated as a woman meant being protected from the hardest work.

"Alright," he said, "come outside with me." We went out to the back deck where Frog was already working in the dense heat and glare. Frog asked to borrow Andres' knife.

"Find yer own knife," replied Andres.

Frog disappeared inside, and came back with a steak knife. Andres put me to work repairing the nets. He showed me how to cut off the raggedy ends and tie the new ends to the existing netting, so that the gaps were closed up. He handed me his knife to use. The knife, a cheap copy of a Buck knife, had "Tomcat" printed on the side of the blade. Preacher also had one, and the two of them sometimes would sit for hours flicking the blades open and shut.

Said Andres, "I let you use this, but not him," he jerked his head in Frog's direction. "He might drop it over the side."

I worked on the nets for a while. They had to be repaired every afternoon before they were set out in the water. Andres picked up a length of chain he wanted cut, and then, pointing to an immense wire cutter on deck, asked me, "You think you can handle that?"

"I'll try." I picked it up and cut the chain. It was hard to cut, but not impossible. Then I worked on cutting and splicing the nets. My hands soon blistered from handling the coarse ropes, but I continued. The afternoon sun beat down and the deck was as hot as a furnace, but I was used to the heat by then. It seemed I could handle this "man's work" well enough. Humming a tune, I put on a pot of spaghetti, and then bandaged my blisters so they wouldn't bother me while I was heading.

Preacher walked into the galley. "Look at your hands," he said. "I gonna call you 'Band-Aid' from now on."

He opened a beer and sat down at the table with it.

Andres walked in. "Well, Pan," he said, "did that work wear you out?"

I shrugged. "It's not that hard."

Andres said, "If we gonna wear you out, it won't be with work, it'll be with fucking. We gonna wear you out with fucking!"

The captain laughed and said, "At least he's honest."

Andres slid over and pressed up against me. "When we gonna start?" he asked.

I pushed him away angrily. "I thought you were gonna treat me like a man. I can't win, can I? Get out of my way now or there won't be any supper."

Once the sauce was simmering, I joined Preacher in the wheelhouse.

"Do you ever get bored out here?" I asked the captain.

"Why . . . you bored?"

"Naw, I haven't been out here long enough for that. I just wondered if you get that way sometimes."

"I'm bored everyday," Preacher responded dryly.

"Yeah?" I contemplated what it would be like to be bored everyday, but to put a good face on it, to go on with your work and joke around with your crew.

"Right now it's not so bad," Preacher continued, "because me an' my present wife are just about washed up. But normally I don't like bein' gone from my family so much. Maybe that's why I've been through so many marriages. You get out of touch, bein' gone so much. You come back after three weeks; you can't just pick up where you left off with your wife and kids. You don't even know where you left off. Then just when you start to get the feelin' of havin' a family again, you have to leave. That hurts. But there's nothin' else I know how to do where I could make the kind of money I need. I don't leave off in the winter like most shrimpers – I shrimp all year round. I'm supportin' three families. Oh, I'd miss the water if I left it, no doubt about that. No matter how you figure it, you can't win."

We were silent for a while, each with our own thoughts. I wondered if I would ever have a family to leave and come home to, or to stay home with. I looked at the glints of light the sun made on the water's surface. They seemed to form a pattern, and soon I was so caught up with watching this pattern that I nearly forget I was looking at the sea. Snapping out of it, I suggested that we watch TV.

"We're too far from shore to pick up any stations," Preacher replied.

"Oh . . . How far out are we?"

"About ninety miles. You didn't even know that, did ya? That's why I'm captain an' you're just a header."

That was the stupidest thing I had ever heard Preacher say. "You're a captain," I pointed out, "because you've been doing this since you were fourteen; this is my first time out."

We ate our supper, and then went out on deck. Preacher had started me on picking up, coiling and replacing the ropes while the rest of the crew was raising or lowering the nets. I could handle the ropes well enough, but I still didn't understand much about the rest of the process. I had no mechanical background to help me, and little practice in using my body vigorously for work or sports; I was at a distinct disadvantage compared to any male deckhand, no matter how green. I thought I could learn in a season, but I didn't know if I would be able to stay on the boat that long.

I was becoming a faster header – since the day of the party I had been heading about as fast as Frog. But two headers weren't really needed on the boat unless the catch was to increase. If Andres and Preacher were to take only one, it would be to their advantage to choose the most experienced header. But it was clear that they liked me, so maybe I would be able to stay.

After the shrimp were headed I moved to the wheelhouse. Preacher was wiggling a Q-tip around in his ear. He held out the box to me. "Wanna screw your ear?" he asked.

I grinned. "Naw. Pretty out tonight, isn't it?"

"Oh . . . It's always pretty out here."

"What'd your name used to be before you were a Preacher?"

"Actually my name is Diego. But they used to call me Loco, 'cause I would do anything on a dare. I'd let people throw knives at me, shoot at me, anything. Once I rode my bike over the levee and stopped it just at the water's edge. But I don't do stuff like that no more. I don' like to fight, but if someone starts something, I will. Now Shades is a mean one in a fight. You wouldn't think it to look at him, 'cause of that baby face of his, but he can fight. Not Andres, now. Andres is all bark an' no bite."

"Figures."

"You know," said Preacher, casting a sly glance my way, "I can't figure you out. Any normal woman out here with three men would be wanting to make it with all of us at once. Yup, that's what a normal woman would do."

I laughed. "That doesn't interest me. Never has."

"I've always had a lot of women after me," said the captain. "After I divorced my second wife I had so many women on my tail, I had the pick of the field. I'm pretty cautious about getting lovey-dovey with a woman – there's too many of 'em in my life already."

I smiled to myself. The silence around us was broken only by the hum of the *Sea Rider*'s engine beneath us, and the slap of water against her hull.

"Once I was in bed with three women," Preacher began again, "but I left without making it with any of 'em. They got in an argument 'bout who was gonna make it with me first, an' I got disgusted and left."

I laughed, wondering if this had really happened. "You've certainly been married enough times. Do you think you'll ever find a woman you can settle down with?"

Preacher shrugged. "Just have to find the right woman."

"Maybe you should marry the sea."

"Ha. Now there's an idea. Although I don't see how I could be anymore married to it than I already am." He paused, and then asked, "Have you ever had any lesbian lovers?"

"Yeah." With some people I would have denied this, but I felt Preacher wouldn't be shocked or hold it against me.

"Did you enjoy it?"

"Sure did."

The captain said, "I know a lot of bi people; nothing wrong with that. I'd like to watch two women get it on."

Ha! I thought to myself, I bet he would.

I shrugged my shoulders. "Did you ever make it with another man?"

"No . . . It just doesn't interest me; I like women. I'd like to go to bed with a real lesbian, the kind that hates men, and show her what it is to be a woman."

I was half amused by his conceit, and half indignant. "That's being a woman, too," I pointed out.

Andres walked into the wheelhouse and sat down on the bleachers next to me.

"Ruthie just told me she's bi," said Preacher. "We gotta find a gay bar for her in Galveston. Maybe she can pick someone up."

I didn't know if I wanted to pick up a woman for the night, but going to a woman's bar in Galveston might be interesting.

"I think we got a magazine around here somewheres," Andres replied casually. "Its got the names of the gay bars."

Andres accepted my bisexuality nonchalantly; he never teased me about it, but just told me about the gay bars in Galveston. Preacher started showing me pictures in the nudie magazines, asking me which ones I liked.

"Ain't these pretty tits?" he asked. "Not too big or too small, nice an' firm."

"They're alright."

The captain said, "I bet you like those skinny-ass women."

"There's more to it than looks," I said. "It's a whole feeling about a person."

"Say whatever you want, but that's one good-lookin' woman."

Hauling up the nets for the second time that night, Preacher handed me a rope to hold by pulling against it. Soon the rope started to move across the deck, carrying me with it. "Drop it, drop the rope!" Preacher and Andres cried out. I pulled my hands away from the moving rope; my body slammed down hard against the deck. If I'd held on just a few seconds more I would have been flung overboard. It was not easy to see a person in the night sea – probably I would have drowned in suffocating terror, or I could have been sucked into the *Sea Rider*'s churning propeller and battered to a pulp.

But none of this happened. Hard as it was, the wooden deck was a comfort beneath me where I had fallen. I could see the deck, the crew, and the sea beyond. I could feel the night breeze and smell the salty spray, and that was all that mattered.

Later on as we were heading the catch, Andres asked me, "Did you hurt yourself when you fell down?"

"Naw. I fell on my ass." Beyond the shock of impact there had been no pain.

"I know," said Andres, "You got lots of padding there."

For a time, we worked at the monotonous heading without speaking. Suddenly, Andres rolled his eyes and yelled, "I'm coming, I'm coming, oh Lord, I'm coming!" Then, in a raspy voice, "Come an' lick it, come an' lick it." He explained, "This bitch said that in a porno film I saw." He tilted his head back, forgetting the shrimp, his basket much fuller than mine or Frog's, and again yelled, "I'm coming, I'm coming, oh Lord, I'm coming."

I was amazed. This man was such a strange mixture of disciplined control, unrestrained emotion, and pure wildness. I had no doubt about his discipline; he took care of a huge amount of work on the boat. As rigman he was responsible for keeping the nets mended, setting them out, and hauling them up. Also he tended the engine, headed shrimp, and took one watch at night so the captain could get some sleep. Before I was hired he also had done the cooking. What he didn't do himself he parceled out to Frog and me, making sure it got done properly. No matter how long he had been working, he always seemed energetic and alert. The exception was night watch, where I had come across him almost nodding off. "I'm very, very tired," he would say, and I could see why.

The work was demanding – if the engine wasn't taken care of properly, the watch not kept, the nets not hauled up just right, our lives would have been in danger. The work came before anything else; we were never too tired to do what needed to be done. The work was done on its own time, as needed, not on our time.

Later Frog woke me from a sound sleep. "I got a cramp in my neck," he said, "Could you rub it for me?" I was half asleep and apprehensive about having Frog in the bunk with me, but he was obviously in pain. I made room for him on the bunk, and worked on his shoulder and neck muscles. Slowly, I felt his muscles relax under my hands, and after a while he said he felt better.

"Let me pay you back," said Frog, and he began to kiss me.

"Forget it!" I pushed him out of the bunk, bristling with anger. Gradually I relaxed and nestled down to sleep some more.

I don't know how long I slept, but I woke suddenly with the feeling that something was wrong. I could feel it, but I didn't know what it was. Standing, moving towards the galley, I sensed the change. The floor was tilted about fifteen degrees off-center, the entire boat was listing to the starboard side. The pattern of the rolling waves, which had become more natural than the stillness of land, had changed. Waves still rolled the *Sea Rider* front to back, but did nothing to right us. Something was wrong, and I struggled to become fully awake, to banish the sleep-numbness from my head.

Then Andres entered the galley. "Don't go out on deck," he cautioned in a subdued voice. "We don't want you to fall overboard. We hit a snag." Without a question or a word I obeyed. Vaguely surprised at his protectiveness, I sat down at the galley table to wait. I had seen snags on the navigation maps – black triangles the boat steered around. How did we get caught? I wondered. Maybe this snag wasn't on the map, or maybe Andres had fallen asleep on watch?

The eerie tilt continued as I wondered what the snag could do to us. Was the boat itself caught? I thought it couldn't be – the water was too deep for that. I figured it must have been the metal cable or the wooden trapdoor at the end of the net that was caught. I wondered if we could free ourselves by cutting the net. It seemed hardly desirable, but maybe it could be done. I didn't know if any tool on board could cut the strong metal cable. Could we radio for help? Maybe the radio wasn't working? No, it must have been working. Preacher and Andres must have been seeing what they could do before radioing for help.

I could see nothing out the galley window. I had known there was a possibility of danger when I had signed on to work this boat. But I also realized that the danger threatened the men working on deck far more than me sitting in the galley - unless the boat was pulled all the way over. Was that possible, I wondered? At any rate, I didn't think the men would fall overboard – their sea legs were too good.

Finally the boat returned to an upright position. Andres came inside and told me that I could come out on deck. We all leaned on the side rail and joked around. Preacher remarked on the size of my biceps muscles. "Flex your arm," he said, "Let's see your muscles." Self-consciously, but with pride, I did so.

"Golly, she got more muscles than a lotta boys do!" Preacher exclaimed. "You know," he continued, changing the subject, "there's not many crews that would be joking around after what just happened."

And he was right. We were a good bunch, it seemed to me.

The others went inside, but I stayed on deck. The night was dark and clear, and by the illumination of our running lights the water sloshed and frothed like volcanic lava before it hardened into rock. I felt relaxed now after the danger and intensity of the night. I breathed in the moist sea air, glad to be alive.

Chapter 8

I woke suddenly because the movement of air had ceased. Frog was crouched next to my bunk. He unplugged my fan and carried it into the next room. I had thought he had a fan too, but apparently his had broken. There were no windows at the level of the lower bunks; without a fan the air was like a suffocating mask, and I didn't see any way I could sleep. I went in to the next bunkroom and unplugged the fan, and then started to carry it out. I felt a twinge of guilt for hogging it, but self-interest won out – I had to have a fan.

"I can't sleep without a fan," said Frog.

"Well neither can I."

"Maybe we should sleep in the same bunk?" he suggested.

"No!"

"You could share Andres' bunk."

"I won't do that!" I snapped at him, louder this time. I wished he had never seen me with Andres – I was sure that was why all of this was happening.

Preacher, sleeping on the top bunk, rolled over and opened his eyes. "What's the problem?" he mumbled.

I didn't want to drag Preacher into this, but it couldn't be helped. I explained, "Frog took my fan and I can't sleep without it."

The captain moved over toward the wall. "You can sleep up here," he said.

Preacher's offer took me totally by surprise. I had the idea that he was someone who maintained a consistent personal space. I would never have expected him to share his bunk, except, of course, with a lover. But I felt OK about the offer; I trusted him completely. He kept a tight rein on his feelings and was concerned about doing what was right, ex-preacher that he was.

So I climbed up into the narrow bunk with him. We tried not to touch each other – which was extremely difficult with only thirty-six inches of space for our two bodies. I attempted to sleep, but sleep would not come, and I had the impression that Preacher was also awake. I didn't feel turned on, but just uncomfortable with the situation. So as not to disturb the man next to me, I lay rigid, unmoving. After several hours of being mostly awake, I got up and stretched out on the floor behind the wheelhouse benches. There was a whisper of a breeze there. The space formed a hard, narrow bed, but I was still not able to sleep.

Shortly afterward, Preacher walked into the wheelhouse. "Getting comfortable down there?" he asked in a smooth, dry voice.

"No." I got up. "Did you get any sleep?"

"Very little."

"Same here. You shouldn't have stood for it," I said, meaning he should have kicked me out.

Preacher took my meaning differently, and said, "You should have made the first move."

Even though I had fantasized about marrying Preacher, making love with him had never occurred to me, not even when I was lying next to him in his bunk. He seemed so closed off, so restrained. Still, sleeping with Andres had taken only the slightest edge off my sexual tension, and I liked Preacher, felt close to him in some ways. I began to consider it.

The captain broke into my musings and said, "I figured out what to do about the fan."

"Yeah?"

"I'm gonna rig my fan up on the wall so it blows on me an' Frog both. He's right – he should have a fan. Then you can have the other one back."

"Sounds good," I said. "I'll be glad to get my fan back – at some point I'm going to need to get some sleep."

Preacher smiled wryly. "I know what you mean . . . Go and wake Andres," he ordered. "It's time for him to get to work. But don't touch him – if you touch him when he's asleep he's liable to hit you."

I woke Andres without touching him. Soon after he walked into the wheelhouse. He and Preacher began talking in Spanish over the CB radio while I started the meal. After a while they walked out to the back deck.

"Shades is on the CB," Preacher said to me in passing. "He wants to talk to you."

I moved to the wheelhouse and picked up the transmitter. "Hello Shades," I said, "What's up over there?"

"These boys still won't cook nothin'," Shades complained in his mellow voice. "If we was closer, I'd come an' have some a that good supper you're cookin'. I know you're boiling up shoe leather."

I laughed. "Yeah, but it smells like steak. Why don't you do your own cooking?"

"I gotta keep the watch. Besides, captains don't cook. Say, sounds like you been havin' lots of excitement over there – what's up?"

I told him about our ship hitting a snag, tilting, and then being righted by the crew. I skimmed over that quickly, and then told him about Frog taking my fan and me sharing Preacher's bunk. As I was talking I realized that hitting the snag was far and away the most important thing that had happened in days, but it didn't feel that way to me. In fact, I'd almost forgotten that it had happened. But I hadn't been involved in doing anything about it, and the pace of events since then had been furious.

I told Shades that I had been up in Preacher's bunk, but we hadn't done anything, just kept each other awake.

He chuckled. "I didn't think you'd share a bunk with one of us dirty Mexicans. Actually, I heard about it already from my brother, but I wanted to hear what you'd say. Now if it'd been me up there, you can bet we woulda done somethin'."

"Ah, but I wouldn't have climbed up in your bunk," I replied.

"When you gonna marry me, Boy?"

"Never."

"I gotta go see about my nets. I talk to you later." Shades signed off.

I returned to the galley and started cutting vegetables for a salad. Andres came in and pressed up against me, one hand clasping my cunt, the other over my breast. I tried to move away, but he held on tight. "What you cookin' up for me, Mamacita?"

I broke free of his hold. "You wanna get fucked in the ass?" I shoved a finger toward his crack.

"You better watch it, Pan." There was anger in Andres' tone, but he got out of my way.

I wondered belatedly if "fighting fire with fire" was the best way to deal with all this. The way to fight a real fire is not with fire, but with water; but I didn't know what would be the water to Andres' teasing. There was no end to his come-ons. In fact, the whole situation was escalating and becoming increasingly difficult to deal with. I didn't enjoy shoving my fingers at Andres' ass; I just wanted to get him off my back. Unable to think of a better solution, I continued to react as I had before, laughing and trading insults with him.

After supper, while the nets were filling, I sat in the wheelhouse with the captain. He was picking out the chords to a new song, "Sixteen Tons," and we sang a bit of it together before he set his guitar aside.

"A trip to Galveston sure would be nice," said Preacher.

"I've been wondering . . . Are shrimpers really as wild when they get into port as they say?"

"Naw. shrimpers talk a lot is all. They'll get drunk, but they don't sleep around nearly as much as they say they do. Take me, for instance. I'll sleep with a woman in port, but it's gotta be the right time an' the right woman."

"Well," I asked, "do you feel the same about women and men sleeping around?"

He thought for a moment, and then said, "As long as a woman has no responsibilities; as long as she isn't married, it's just the same."

"And what if a man's married?"

"When he starts playing around, that's when he knows it's time to leave." The room was silent, and then Preacher asked, "Well, do you want to make it with me? If so, all you have to do is make a move."

That took me by surprise. A small stirring inside me said yes. "I'm not sure," is what I actually said. "I'm afraid I might not like it, and you'd keep wanting to. I like to make love with a lot of touching – I like it to be sensual. But I have to admit I'm kind of horny."

Preacher chuckled. "Why didn't you get Andres to help you out?" he asked. "He's certainly willing."

"Well, first I didn't have any birth control. Then I got some foam in Galveston."

He asked, "Is that what you did that morning before we left the harbor?"

"Yeah," I admitted. "But I never did make it with Andres because he wouldn't do what I wanted; he's not into touching. That's too bad – I like him. He has a beautiful body." Part lie, part truth.

"Well," said Preacher, "I take it the way it comes. I think we should sleep together, if only to relieve the tension."

That made sense to me, and relieved my fears about any coercion being involved, but not my fears about the quality of the experience.

By now everyone on the boat was preoccupied with sex. Preacher had started teasing Frog, telling him to bend over and he'd ream him. I thought that talk was ugly, but Frog took it in good humor, saying he was turned on, shaking his arms and saying, "I'm coming!"

Once I had decided to sleep with Preacher, I could think of nothing else. My skin tingled with a kind of sexual electricity. Every hour the charge increased. Having been invited to his bed, I went as soon as everyone was asleep, waking him up by gently shaking his arm.

"What's up?" he asked.

"Can I come up there with you?"

Preacher shook his head. "Not now, I gotta get some sleep. Later, maybe on watch tonight."

So I went back to my own bunk, feeling abashed, and noiselessly used my fingers to get myself off.

That night Andres and Frog went to sleep while the nets were dragging. The hour was late, a lost hour of the night.

Preacher turned out the lights in the wheelhouse, grabbed roughly at my tits, and then asked, "Is this the kind of foreplay you like? . . . Now don't try to kiss me; I don't even kiss my wife – got a set of false teeth."

He unzipped his cut-offs and guided me down. I was aware of a musky odor and crinkly hairs against my face. I knew he wouldn't do this for me, but I felt like doing it, so took him in my mouth. Soon he lifted me up. "You better stop, or I'll come before we even get started."

All the while Preacher was sitting in the captain's chair, keeping the watch. He pulled down my shorts and panties and pulled me up to straddle him. He felt good, so good in me, but the position was all wrong;

because of the armrests on the chair I couldn't move my hips against him the way I wanted.

Only a small part of this man was with me, I could feel that. The majority of his attention was on the boat – the location of possible snags, the position of other crafts around us. With the part of him that was there, Preacher shot his seed into me. I could easily have started over, but Preacher patted me on the butt and said, "I gotta go check the try net for Andres; keep the watch for me, OK?" We disengaged our bodies, and then Preacher went out to the back deck.

I pulled on my clothes and sat in the captain's chair to keep watch. I felt forlorn, shaken by the coldness of the encounter. With the lights out, the stars were magnificent bright points in the dark sky. I felt so alone beneath it.

The captain returned from the back deck. "I think there's enough shrimp to pull up the nets," he said evenly. "I'll go wake Andres and Frog." He switched on the lights.

I put some water on to boil, grabbed my crusted, fishy-smelling work pants and boots from the side rail, and put them on. I drank some tea while Frog and Andres got ready, and then we all trooped out to the back deck, which was brightly lit like a stage set. With their dark features and deliberate motions, the crew resembled samurai, the Japanese warriors of ancient times. Andres with his strong limbs, brooding features, and massive, dark hair pulled back would be our samurai leader. Preacher with his deliberate karate motions at the ropes was unquestionably the martial arts master. Frog and I were the novices, still being tested.

One of the nets got tangled coming up, so Andres scrambled out on a cable over the side, and then crouched down to unhook it – something I'd be petrified to do. Then two huge pear-shaped nets loomed over the deck. Preacher went back to the wheelhouse as Frog and Andres walked up to the nets, grabbing a rope end in each hand. They pulled the ropes alternately, something like milking a cow, until the knots gave way and a mass of squirming sea-things dropped to the deck, spreading out in every direction.

We grabbed push brooms and raked the catch into one central pile. Shoving on our gloves, grabbing low stools and rakes, we grouped ourselves around the edges of the pile and began the tedious process of heading. Dismissing Preacher from my mind, I concentrated on working as fast as I could. Andres grabbed a good shrimp that I'd missed out of my scrap pile. Frowning, he held it up, and then threw it back in front of me.

A little while later I found a shrimp with a tag attached to its body. I knew what it was. The tags were used to study the crustacean's life cycle and migrations. There was a reward offered for some of them. I showed the tagged shrimp to Andres. "I show this to Preacher," he said, and took it inside. He came back without it. I figured he was going to take credit for it, and get the reward if there was one. I brooded for a little while, and then decided it wasn't worth getting upset over. We finished heading in silence. I helped sweep the junk fish off the deck, and then staggered inside to nap while Andres and Frog iced down the catch.

I pulled my clothes and boots off my dirty, sweaty body, left them by the rail, and then clambered into my bunk. Rocked by the ship's motion, I was asleep in no time.

I awoke to the feeling of drops of water splashing on my face. Andres, crouched by my bunk, said in a gentle voice, "Wake up, Mamacita. We gotta head the third catch." Andres had been keeping the night watch for the past few hours. He should have been exhausted, but he seemed filled with energy.

We sat in the galley, joking around and smoking for a few minutes before going out to the deck. It helped to be fully awake before hauling up the nets. The first light of approaching dawn was visible over the water, which was relatively calm. The nets were raised and we crouched down to head an enormous catch. Clearly we would be heading for a long time. As I worked I stole glances at the dawn. The sky became paler and paler. A few clouds low in the sky took on a pink tinge. Finally the amber tip of the sun spread a line of molten gold over the water at the easternmost rim of the horizon, and then rose higher, ever higher, in the sky. Andres unfurled awnings to shade us as we worked.

Preacher came out and assisted with the heading for a bit. Then he put his basket aside and said, "I'm gonna pull rank on you all." He stood by the rail, threw cans in the water, and shot them full of holes as they bobbed on the waves.

"Can I try that sometime?" I asked.

"I thought you didn't like to kill things," said Preacher.

"I don't, but I like to shoot. I tried it once before."

"After breakfast you can try it. Hey, Andres, come look at these redfish."

Andres moved over to the rail, and then quickly returned to the catch pile and searched out a squid. He baited a length of line with it, hurled it over the side, and then after a brief struggle landed a fish about two feet long. He baited another line and hooked a second fish. This one put up quite a struggle. Preacher stood behind Andres and wrapped muscular arms around his waist to prevent him from losing his footing.

Working together, they landed a huge fish. As it thrashed about madly on the planking, Andres laughed and said, "That redfish almost pulled me overboard. These fish is good to eat. We have the little one for supper; I'm gonna sell the big one." He went back to heading shrimp, singing in a raucous voice as he worked.

By the time we finished heading the sun was burning fiercely in a pale sky. The waves sparkled with points of light, rolling and pitching, throwing salty spray on the *Sea Rider*'s flanks. I went in to start breakfast, but after a little while Preacher called me back outside.

The deck had been washed down with seawater. Everyone was getting soaked under the hose and was washing with a shared bar of soap on deck – unlimited showers. Preacher hosed me down. With soaked clothes clinging to our bodies we all played in the water, taking turns spraying each other, laughing and fighting over the hose. It felt so good to be clean and wet that somehow the saltiness of the water didn't bother us.

After we ate the captain took me out to the side rail, where he showed me how to aim and shoot his gun.

"Now this is gonna kick after you fire it," he warned me. "Don't let go." He showed me how to aim and squeeze the trigger, and then threw a can into the waves for me to practice on. Holding the pistol with both hands, I aimed and shot.

"Oh," I gasped, surprised at the violence of the blast.

"At least you didn't drop the gun," Preacher commented approvingly.

I shot a few more times, finally hitting one of the cans. Then, my lack of sleep caught up with me and I moved to my bunk, where I gladly gave up consciousness for a time.

I awoke before anyone else that afternoon. Moving my fan into the wheelhouse, I sat in the captain's chair to smoke and think, enjoying being the only one awake.

For the first time since it had happened, I turned my thoughts to my encounter with Preacher the night before. It was difficult for me to accept the coldness of the relationship. I was all wound up with needs: different but intertwining needs for sex, warmth, affection, and a respite from the increasing hysteria on board. My feelings were like a tightly-stretched cord. They vibrated easily; they could have snapped easily.

Whatever else it lacked, our coupling had been fairly satisfying on a physical level, and I was too strung out not to want to continue.

In one way I saw the lack of emotion in the relationship as an advantage – no tension was placed on our working relationship. This was crucial to Preacher and important to me. We worked together as if nothing had happened – and emotionally nothing had.

I picked up a magazine and leafed through it idly. Frog walked in and sat down on the bench. "It's hot today," he commented.

I shrugged. "It's always hot."

"When I get home," said Frog, "I'm gonna buy a present for my little niece. She's only four, but she's really cute . . . I'm crazy about her."

"Children are great," I responded. "I love my sister's kid – she looks a lot like me – but I don't get to see her much because they live on the East Coast." Frog was so different from Preacher and Andres. They never talked about their children, never showed that soft side of themselves.

"D'you want to trade back rubs?" he asked. "My neck's botherin' me again . . . I can give one, too – I'm pretty good at it."

I smiled. "You won't bother me like you did the last time?"

"Naw, I won't get into nothin' with you."

"OK." I fetched the sheet from my bunk and spread it out over the narrow carpeted space behind the benches. Frog lay down and I worked on his neck, shoulders and back. His skin felt velvety. I could feel his muscles unknot under my fingers.

When it was my turn, I removed my shirt and lay on my stomach on the sheet. Frog turned out to be surprisingly competent. His touch was gentle and sensitive. I wondered what it would be like to sleep with him. He was nowhere near as interesting as the captain or the rigman. But it occurred to me now that he might be a far more sensitive and satisfying lover than either of them. Nevertheless, I dismissed the possibility from my thoughts. Frog's status on the boat was so low; I felt mine would be equally low, or lower, if I shared his bunk.

The massage ended. True to his word, Frog hadn't made a pass at me this time, for which I was grateful. We sat in the wheelhouse and exchanged small talk until Frog went out to work on the deck with Andres, and I moved into the galley to start supper.

Preacher stood beside me for a few moments. "You know," he said, his voice low, "Andres asked me why we had the lights out last night. Andres is nobody's fool. I don't want him findin' out about us."

"What'd you tell him?"

I said we were just lookin' at the stars is all. I think he believed me."

"Well I don't want Andres to find out either," I said, "but I would like to sleep with you again."

Preacher grinned. "You mean you're ready for 'Freddy'?"

"Oh, I'm ready; I'm more than ready!" I continued cooking. The captain moved to the wheelhouse, a copy of *Penthouse* in his hand.

Chapter 9

After we'd had sex, Preacher treated me differently than before. He started teasing me, and picked up Andres' habit of calling me "pan." Actually his teasing was different from Andres'. Gentler and more humorous, it included me rather than shutting me out, so that, except for his calling me "pan," I didn't mind it.

What bothered me was not the teasing, but rather that Preacher would no longer talk to me on any other level. It didn't matter what I tried to talk about, he either responded in monosyllables, or twisted the topic around to sex. Given the choice, I would rather have had our friendship back and skipped the sex, but I saw no way for that to happen. I mourned our serious, thoughtful relationship, which was no more.

What with the time and energy that our work demanded, and the need for secrecy, two days elapsed before I slept with Preacher again – this time in his bunk. He turned me so that I was facing away from him, and then entered me from behind. I was washed in waves of feeling – feeling centered in my female core and radiating outward.

Afterwards, as we were lying there, Preacher said, "I bet you didn't think to put in your foam in this time."

"I put it in before I came in here. I have to think about it – no one else is going to."

"That's true." Preacher checked his watch, and then said, "Look, I don't mean to be rude, but it's 4 a.m., and I have to get some sleep. You can stay up here with me if you want. I really don't care anymore if Andres knows we're doing this. To hell with 'im." The captain rolled over and was asleep almost instantly.

I stayed in his bunk for a while. Outside it was raining hard. There was a sudden loud clap of thunder. I didn't move, but Preacher jumped.

"You ain't even scared of the storm, are you?" he asked.

I shook my head. "I like the rain and the thunder."

"Well, I have to look out for my boat," he said, getting out of bed to check on Andres in the wheelhouse.

I did like the storm – the strong, clean feeling of water slashing against the deck, and sinking as if to home in the dark sea; the powerful jagged flashes of bluish light, and the sudden roars and rumbles as the air was superheated, and then ripped apart by electric energy.

A hurricane would have frightened me, but the storm excited me.

The storm subsided. Preacher had returned to bed and sank back to sleep; I slipped out of his bunk and into my own. He may not have cared whether or not Andres knew about us, but I cared; I was the one Andres would take it out on.

When I woke in the afternoon, the air was blessedly cool. Outside a misty rain was falling. I got up and walked out on deck, wearing only my panties. Semi-undressed, with the unusual coolness and the fine touch of rain, I felt like I was floating. Mirroring the sky, the sea looked gray and cool. The universe was perfect.

Walking inside I found Andres staring at me from his bunk. "You must think you look pretty that way," he commented coldly.

I shrugged. "The rain feels good." My elevated mood had been shattered. I threw on the rest of my clothes and started the evening meal.

Preacher came into the galley and asked, "What's for supper, Pan?"

Pan – cunt – the hated nickname Andres had given me; a name Preacher had recently started to use as well.

"Can I talk to you seriously for a minute?" I asked.

"What's up?"

"Promise not to tell Andres?"

"OK"

"I wish you wouldn't call me pan. I don't like Andres doing it, either, but I figure if I told him that, it would just make things worse."

Preacher asked, "Do you know what 'pan' means?"

"Yeah."

"It means 'bread.' "

"That's not the point, Preacher."

He chuckled. "So you don't like bein' called 'pan'? You still never told me what's for supper."

"Chicken."

"Umm, some fried chicken, that sounds good."

Andres walked into the galley. "You better not ruin that chicken, Pan," he threatened me.

"Hey, man," said Preacher, "You better not call her 'pan' – she told me she don' like it."

"Too bad if she don' like it," Andres tossed off between gritted teeth.

I was breading the chicken. There was a sinking feeling in the pit of my stomach. It was difficult for me to believe that Preacher would have betrayed my confidence as he just did. It seemed the name of the game was never to take yourself too seriously, and it must be played to the hilt – always. I felt like a rat in a maze, with no way out.

I was angry and disappointed in Preacher, who I had thought was my friend, someone to be trusted. I still liked him, but some quality was gone. I'd always known that sleeping with men I was working with was a mistake, but the body has its own knowledge, which it's difficult to ignore.

That night my mind wandered while I was working on deck, and I failed to coil the ropes out of the way when I was supposed to. The captain came over and stood beside me with his hands on his hips. Abandoning his habitual control, he let flow a torrent of abuse. "Motherfucker, cocksucker, son-of-a-bitch, fucking incompetent idiot, goddamn! Why the hell don't you watch what you're doing?"

Maybe it was because I was spaced out, maybe it was because of some quality of the way he delivered this, but I felt strangely divorced from the words, like they somehow were aimed at my actions, but not at me. His words floated over my shoulder and out into space. At the end of his tirade Preacher said, "I'm sorry to yell at you like that, Ruthie, but dammit, you gotta watch what you're doin'."

There was nothing I could reply to that, but somehow the whole incident, my action and the captain's reaction, seemed tangled up with the change in our relationship.

We finished bringing in the catch, headed the shrimp, iced them down, and then traipsed inside.

Andres came up to me. "I bet you don't even want to go out there again," he said sympathetically.

"No," I replied, "I just want to go out there and do better."

The boat work had its own rhythm, and the whirl of activity carried me swiftly through the next two days. I made an effort to be alert on deck, and there were no more complaints about my work. The life and the work went on: cooking, eating, and sleeping; keeping watch; mending, setting out, and pulling up the nets; heading and icing down the shrimp; cleaning the deck – an endless, round-the-clock routine.

Above and beyond our human round of activities were the cycles and changes of the natural world. The shifting of the waves was a constant, but the intensity varied. The cycle of shifting light, day and night went on, with variations in the clouds, the colors at sunrise and sunset, the fullness of the moon, and the brightness of the stars.

On the surface, my relationships with the other crewmembers stayed about the same. I spent very little time with Frog, who quietly went about his work. Andres alternated between periods of being sweet and considerate toward me, and bouts of teasing, which were becoming more and more outrageous. Preacher continued to joke around with me, but our former intimacy of friendship was gone. There was an understanding between us that we would continue to sleep together from time to time.

Along with the sameness of routine, emotional tension was building on the boat. Sex had become virtually the only topic of conversation, and Frog and I were being teased almost constantly. There were still times when I enjoyed being with the crew, but I was disappointed with the change in my relationship with Preacher, and I became increasingly impatient with Andres' teasing.

Being on a boat, living and working in the same small space, there was no way to take time out from the situation at hand. It was physically impossible to take a day or an evening off – to go to a movie, to fly a kite, or to talk to a sympathetic friend. Any tension became exaggerated, more so each day.

After breakfast one morning I joined the captain and the rigman in the wheelhouse while Frog took his turn at washing the dishes. We were all joking around, unwinding from the night's work.

"Hey, Ruthie," asked Preacher, "are you ticklish?"

"No," I lied.

"Let's find out." Andres pinned my arms behind me so I couldn't defend myself as Preacher tickled me and grabbed a feel of my breasts. I giggled and tried to get away. After a minute they let me go.

"Thought you said you weren't ticklish," commented Preacher.

"I never tell anyone."

"Um," said Andres, "From now on we gonna tie you up and tickle you everyday."

"I'll find me another boat if you do that."

We continued sitting in the wheelhouse, making small talk and joking around. I was disturbed that Andres had held me down, but I didn't say anything about it, acting as if everything was OK. Later Preacher held my arms down so Andres could tickle me, and that made matters worse.

After the rest of the crew had gone to sleep, I continued sitting in the wheelhouse. I was seething with suppressed anger, and I no longer knew how far to trust these men. It felt like they were ganging up on me; the next time I feared they would hold me down and rape me. I didn't think they would, but I no longer knew what to think. Anger was swelling in me; I had to release it somehow. I took the wheelhouse cushions out to the front deck, as far away as I could get from the rest of the crew, and started beating on them.

The boat was a small space, and so everyone was soon aware of what I was doing. Frog came out first. "Are you flipping out?" he asked.

"No!" I continued to beat the cushions.

Soon after that the captain came out. Standing a few feet away from me, he asked, "Why are you beating on my pillows? Can't we talk about it?"

I stopped and looked at him. "I'm mad because you and Andres held me down. It feels like you're ganging up on me."

"If we were really ganging up on you," Preacher pointed out, "it would be different."

"I know, but it feels that way."

"If something's bothering you, come talk to me about it – but don't beat on my pillows anymore."

Sure I'll talk to him about it, I thought. Like the time I asked him not to call me pan and he kept on doing it, and even told Andres.

The captain asked, "Do you want me to tell Andres to stop teasing you? He thinks you like it."

I was shocked. Andres thought I like being teased? Of course I had laughed and exchanged insults with him – it had seemed to be the only way of dealing with the situation. But I hated it. It felt like a constant war, kept at the level of minor skirmishes.

"Well I don't like it," I snapped. "If you can get him to stop, go right ahead."

"I'll tell him to stop. You feel OK now?"

I didn't feel OK, but I nodded yes. The captain went back inside. My feelings were all churned up; feelings I had kept a tight lid on before this. Sitting on one of the cushions, I started to cry.

Preacher came back out. "What's wrong now?" he asked.

"I just feel like crying."

Incredulous, he shook his head. "No one should ever cry," he told me, "an' particularly not on a boat. Christ, there's enough water out here already." He walked back inside.

Finally I got the message that what I was doing was beyond the pale in the crew's eyes. I forced myself to stop crying, moved inside, and tried to sort out my feelings. Suddenly I recalled an experience which helped to explain my violent reaction to being held down. . . .

The time was maybe five years before. I was in Mexico, traveling in the mountains by bus – solo. From one village I needed to take a cab to the train station, several miles away.

The bus driver found a cab for me. He and a younger man got in along with the driver. I had a premonition of danger, but let it go. We drove out into the desert, and then the driver stopped the car. They all jumped on me, took turns holding me down, and one at a time they raped me. I struggled the whole time (and had black and blue marks for days afterwards), but I was powerless to stop them. They laughed and said it was "sabrosa" – the Spanish word meaning "tasty." The word has always nauseated me since.

Finally I fled to a nearby village; my attackers didn't pursue me. I don't know how I found the place. Coming out of the desert into its one dusty street was like walking into a dream. The street was lined with mud houses. The people, too, seemed of the earth. Several sat on front stoops, listening to mariachi music from an ancient radio. Loud, rhythmic, and plaintive, the music filled the night. Crying silently, I told them what had happened. One woman warmed up some tortillas and beans for me and offered me a straw mat to sleep on in her hut. She lay down on a larger mat beside her husband. They slept in their clothes, without covers. I remember being cold and feeling my bruises against the hard mat. . . .

* * *

Having figured out this connection between present and past, I felt much calmer. Moving to my bunk, I shed my clothes and fell soundly asleep.

I felt better when I woke up, but not for long. The atmosphere on the boat had changed drastically. No one teased me, but they barely talked to me at all. I had thought that without the teasing the atmosphere on the boat would return to the camaraderie of the first few days. Of course that was impossible – too many things had happened since then; there was no going back.

To my horror I even missed the teasing; it was certainly better than this cold silence. I decided to have a few days of peace and quiet, and then tell Andres that he could tease me if he wanted. Actually he had already started, just a bit here and there. There was really no stopping him. I wished I could talk things out with the crew, but that seemed impossible.

One day we were all standing around and Preacher asked Frog, "What would you do if we had some pussy on the boat?"

"We have some," said Frog, nodding in my direction.

"No," the captain shook his head, "we don't have any."

Frog looked at Preacher and said, "If we had some pussy, I'd get on top of it and fuck it."

I stood there silently, feeling all torn up inside, curiously visible and invisible at the same time.

Suddenly the shrimp disappeared, and I recalled the old belief that a woman on a boat is bad luck. It was as if the sea creatures could sense the charged atmosphere on the boat and kept their distance. For the past few nights, as we steered a course toward Galveston, we had been catching only enough shrimp to boil and eat as a midnight snack. This, of course, did nothing for morale.

We again entered Galveston harbor, and none too soon. Spirits were low; everyone needed a break from life on the boat.

Once we were inside the harbor, Andres approached Frog and me and said, "You can see there ain't enough work for two headers, so I'm gonna keep the one that does the most work." Clearly that was Frog; I had been fired.

My head spun. Despite everything negative that had happened, despite the tension on board, I still wanted to stay on the boat, still thought things could get better, given a little time. Preacher and Andres hadn't treated me very well the previous two days. Still, I felt a kind of sisterly love toward them, something stronger than any sexual feeling. I had expected to stay on the boat – at least until this voyage was completed – and I was not prepared to put these men, this boat, this living and working on the water, out of my life.

As I stood in the wheelhouse brooding, Preacher came up to me. "I'm sorry we couldn't take you back with us, Ruthie," he said, "but you freaked me out the other day – I'm afraid of what you might do if we keep you."

"I wasn't freaking out."

"You know, after you beat on the cushions, I started sleeping with my gun under my pillow."

"Really?" I was incredulous. "I'd never hurt any of you."

The captain shrugged. "You did good for a beginner," he said, and then quickly left the wheelhouse. This time I didn't believe him; the words sounded like a formula recited to dismiss the situation. Oh, I had done well enough for a beginner at the actual work, but I messed up in other ways: by telling Andres about my dream, by beating on the pillows and actually crying on deck, by allowing sexual feelings to enter into a work situation.

Moodily, I wandered back to the deck and watched the shrimp being unloaded. Two Coast Guard officials came on board and Andres gave them the tagged shrimp, along with the boat's bearings at the time I had found it. He told them that he had found it, giving them his name and address in case there was a reward. I watched all this in silence, hoping that there would be no reward, that Andres would get nothing out of it.

I stepped off the boat and walked toward the harbor road, thinking as I went. It had been decent of Preacher to tell me the real reason for my termination; he hadn't had to. I kept wishing I'd never beat on the pillows. If only . . . if only I could change what had already happened. But this wishing was pointless. I decided to try to persuade Preacher to rehire me. I walked down the same street I had the last time we were in Galveston – a forlorn replica of the same walk.

Returning to the boat, I asked Preacher if there was any way I could stay. He pondered a moment, and then said, "You'll have to ask Andres."

I knew this game. If I asked Andres, he would tell me to ask Preacher. I resolved to ask him, anyway. But Andres was not on the boat, and before he returned Preacher came back to where I was standing and said, "I'm sorry, Ruthie, but that's the way it is. Anyway, you see how the shrimp are running." He wrote me a check for my share of the catch and gave me bus fare back to Aransas Pass. "Wait till my buddy Jose shows up, and we'll give you a ride to the bus station," he offered.

So I packed my clothes. Andres returned and I shook hands with him and Frog, a ritualized, masculine farewell. Goodbyes are strange anyway, and this one was stranger than most. Whatever had bonded me to this crew had come unglued . . . hopelessly unglued.

The captain and his friend drove me to the bus station. The last thing Preacher said to me was: "Don't ever let anyone know what you're feeling. That way they can't hurt you."

The advice was appropriate to the situation, and summed up Preacher's philosophy neatly. But I knew I would never live that way unless I was forced to do so by a repressive, prison-type situation. Invulnerability is a self-imposed prison; a person has to be hurt many times before he or she gets to that point. I felt sad that this had happened to Preacher. He was a beautiful person, and I would miss him. Already I missed the *Sea Rider* and her crew.

Chapter 10

After I arrived at the station, I boarded the bus for Aransas Pass. I overheard a passenger talking about cooking on oil rigs. Interested, I moved back to where he was sitting. I told him I'd been working on a shrimper and wanted to try cooking on a rig. We exchanged names – his was Alfredo.

Alfredo was a small man dressed in slacks and a cotton-knit shirt. "I'm just going back to work," he told me in a soft, high-pitched voice. "I been sick for a while. They arranged this job special for me – I have to be at the spot where the helicopter's going to pick me up by 1:00 a.m. I don't know if I'm gonna make it," he fretted. Abruptly he stopped talking and looked hard at me. "Are you a girl or a guy?" he asked.

"What's it to you?"

"No offense, I just wondered."

"I'm a woman."

Alfredo shook his head. "A shrimp boat is no place for a girl. You get yourself a cooking job on a rig – that'll be better."

"I like boats," I protested. "But I would like to work on a rig someday."

"The thing about rig work," Alfredo said, "is to get the roughnecks to be your friends – that way you won't have no trouble. Me, I never have to do no heavy work. If there's a sack of potatoes to be moved, one of the roughnecks does it for me. It's clean work, too. I can wear my good clothes – I never get dirty."

In Houston we had to go to another station to transfer buses. Since we were both going, we decided to take a cab together. As we stood on the street corner, Alfredo let a cab go by.

"Why didn't you flag it down?" I asked.

Alfredo's eyes flicked briefly over three men standing just down the street from us. "I don't want to call a cab until those guys leave. They might think we have something valuable in these suitcases, and try to rip us off."

A wave of irritation swept over me. Unlike Alfredo, I wasn't afraid to be on the street. I found myself thinking, "I'm more of a man than he is." As soon as I thought this, I was appalled. Like the world around me, I was equating masculinity with courage, and femininity with weakness. I thought I had obliterated that type of thinking from my mind long ago. I did feel I was a stronger person than Alfredo, but was I "more of a man"?

I flagged down the next cab, and we rode to the station.

As my sexual prejudices appeared, although unvoiced, Alfredo began to voice his. "Why d'you dress like that?" he asked, indicating my jeans and T-shirt. "You'd look much better in a dress."

Through gritted teeth I replied, "I'm not gonna work in a dress, for chrissake!"

Alfredo persisted in trying to change my life and my style. Finally he looked at me mournfully and asked, "Why don't you quit working on boats and come home to Galveston with me?" He began pleading with me, disregarding my protests that I wasn't interested.

At last I blew up. "Just get away from me," I growled, "I don't want to have anything else to do with you." He left me alone until I was in line to board the bus, and then he slipped in beside me.

"I just want us to be friends," he pleaded.

"Don't stand by me, and don't sit near me," I hissed. I was aware of amusement and embarrassment in the crowd. I felt like I was living a replay of *Bus Stop*, but at the same time I found the situation vaguely funny. At least, I was aware that it would seem funny to me later. Finally Alfredo left me alone. I got on the bus to Aransas Pass and promptly fell asleep.

My transition to life on land took several days, during which time I would wake up at night to see the entire room swinging to and fro. Mostly I rested, physically and mentally, from my life aboard the *Sea Rider*. A tropical storm blew in, so I delayed looking for work on another trawler.

The two weeks I'd spent on the shrimper had been the most intense of my life, and I wanted to go right back out on another boat – to be in touch with the elements, to test my endurance, and to master the nets. I wanted to stay with one boat for the rest of the season. That might be possible if I could find the right crew, and avoid the mistakes I'd made on the *Sea Rider*.

When the weather improved, I walked the docks looking for work. Because of the storm, the shrimp boats were lined up three deep in the harbor, more boats than I'd ever seen in one place. Many were from other ports; there was even one from Oregon. The *Sea Rider* was there, and also Shades' boat, the *Miss B*, but both were empty of their crews.

I got a job offer from a captain named Jose on a boat out of Brownsville. When I told him I intended to bunk alone, he said, "We have a fourth bunk, but it's full of stuff. You could clean it out if you want." I left to get my clothes. When I returned he told me he'd changed his mind about hiring me, and then asked, "How come you don't want to sleep with me?"

Disgusted, I continued walking the dock. The next time I got around to where his boat was, he beckoned to me. "Come on, get your clothes. Two of my crew just quit me, and I have to get a crew together."

I laughed. "Forget it," I said, "I ain't gonna work for you."

By this point I had pretty much decided to give up on shrimping and head for New Orleans, where I had friends. I no longer had the energy to spend days walking the dock, looking for work. Besides, I was feeling pretty lonely – I needed to be around folks I knew. I walked around to the *Miss B*, and this time Shades was there. I asked Shades about working for him.

He shook his head and said, "My boat's too small, only three bunks." Then he asked, "How come you're not on Preacher's boat no more?"

"I got mad one day and beat on some pillows out on the deck."

Shades roared with laughter, and then became serious, asking, "What'd you get mad about?"

"They were holding me down to tickle me. I didn't like being held down."

"Did it bother you when you were played with like that before?"

This man has a sharp mind, I thought. I didn't want to get into that, so instead I asked him, "Do you think what I did was crazy?"

He thought a minute, and then said, "I wouldn't expect a grown woman to act like that. A three-year-old, yes, but not a grown woman. But I don't think you're crazy, except in the way that I'm crazy, too. Preacher, he's crazy same as us; Andres is crazy in a little different way. Now Frog . . ." here Shades shook his head, "Frog is somethin' else again."

No doubt about it, I thought, being crazy was definitely a compliment.

Shades said, "I already seen Preacher and them, an' they told me about it. I wanted to hear what you'd say."

"They thought I would try to kill them or something. Preacher even slept with his gun under his pillow afterwards. He told me that after they fired me. I didn't want to hurt them – that's why I just beat on the pillows."

Shades chuckled, and then tapped me on the arm. "Let's go get a beer," he said.

We went to a waterfront bar owned by Shades' cousin, who was bartending. The dim coolness was in sharp contrast to the bright Texas sunshine outside. We sat at the bar and talked over drinks.

"I sure wish I could work on your boat," I said.

Shades shook his head. "I can't take you, Boy. My rigman's a Christian – he'd never go for it."

"You let your rigman tell you what to do?"

"I can do without a extra header an' cook, but I need my rigman. Besides, you wouldn't like it on my boat. If I took a woman out it would be for sex, not work. I'd try it the first night, an' if it didn't work out, I'd bring her right back the next day. If I kept her on the boat, once I got tired of her, I'd pass her on to my rigman, an' after that to my header.

If Shades was trying to talk me out of working on his boat, he'd certainly done it. "Damn, Shades," I said, "I like the way your brother thinks about women better. He accepts people for what they are and what they can do; he doesn't judge them based on what sex they are."

"Why don't you accept being a woman?" he asked. "You can't go out there an' do the work a man does."

I had no complete answer for this. Thinking I was "more of a man" than Alfredo had made me realize that I wasn't clear in my head as to how I saw myself and what I wanted. But at least I was working on it. I told Shades, "I want to be seen as a person first, then as a woman."

Shades nodded, "I think I can see you that way."

I thought he could, too, or I wouldn't have been sitting there talking to him. I was drinking greyhounds – vodka and grapefruit juice. As soon as I finished one, another would appear in front of me.

Shades leaned over towards me and asked, "Do you like sitting next to a big man like me?"

"What? I don't care if you're big or not – I just like being around you."

His eyes sparkling, Shades said, "I'm gonna get you drunk and seduce you."

"You don't have to get me drunk."

"Naw," he shook his head, "I was just foolin'."

Andres came in and stood next to us at the bar. He had lost weight and his fine mane of hair was clean and brushed. "H'lo Pan," he nodded in my direction.

Bastard, I thought, and felt my face redden, but the light was too dim in the bar for anyone to notice.

Andres said, "You know, Frog quit workin' for us after you left; we really needed you."

"You make it sound like I quit. I was willing to work then, and I'll still work, if you'll take me back."

Andres took a swig of his beer, and then said, "You'll have to talk to Preacher. . . . If you came back it would be worse. You really freaked out." Disbelief raised the pitch of his voice. "You were cryin' an' everything!"

"I didn't freak out – I just got angry is all."

"One thing I'd like to know," Andres asked, "Why wouldn't you make it with me after that one time?"

I couldn't believe he'd brought that up. But since I wasn't on the crew anymore, there was no need for discretion from his point of view. This was my opportunity to put him in his place, and he had asked for it. "You had your chance," I said, "You wouldn't do what I wanted."

Shades, a born gossip, had been following the conversation closely. His eyes dancing, he said, "Just in and out, in and out, that's no fun."

Andres grumbled, "I was asleep; you shouldn't have come up there when I was asleep." He then left to go sit at one of the tables.

Shades said, "I heard what you said to Andres – that made sense."

"Well," I reflected, "I guess he really wasn't very awake."

"Oh, no," Shades responded vehemently, "You're awake when you go to make it with somebody!"

A youngish man with long blond hair and a beard entered the bar and approached us.

"Where you been, man?" he asked Shades, irritation clearly discernible in his voice. "I been waitin' at your house for hours to see about fixin' your bike."

"Are you angry?" Shades asked.

"Damn right I'm angry. Here I was gonna do you a favor, an' you don't even show up."

"I tell you what, man. If you're that upset about it, you can have the bike."

"Naw," said the hippie, "I couldn't take your bike. I just wish you'd shown up when you'd say you were gonna, is all."

"I got hung up talkin' to this lady. Buy you a drink?"

"Some other time. I gotta git goin'," he said, and then walked out of the bar.

The attitude behind Shades' words was clear and familiar from my two weeks on the boat: Don't take yourself too seriously.

We drifted over to a table where some boat people Shades knew were sitting. Shades introduced me to Luis, a captain from Brownsville.

"Ask him for a job," Shades said, nudging me with his elbow. "I'll give you a recommendation. I'll tell him your biscuits are hard as rocks." We all laughed.

Luis said, "I'd give you a job, but I got a full crew."

Preacher walked in and sat down at our table. He looked smaller, less impressive than he had on board. "Hello, Ruthie," he said, and then ignored me.

Shades nudged me. "Ask him for your job back," he whispered. I shook my head. Clearly my old job was a lost cause. Besides, what Andres had said was true – if I came back, things would be worse.

Luis invited me to spend the night with him, and I refused. He and Shades launched into a discussion about a woman Shades had slept with the night before, about whether Shades had "hurt her." I couldn't understand what they were talking about. I started to have the strange feeling that I was sitting here with my past, and I had an overpowering need to get out of this dim, smoky bar, to be on the beach. After saying goodbye, I headed for the ferry to Port Aransas.

With the purity of the sand, the wind and the now-dark sea surrounding me, I sat down to think. Working on the boat I had pushed against barriers, moved away from safe harbors into the new and unknown. But like the catch, which had cascaded over the deck when the giant nets were opened, I'd been picked up, transported, and abruptly dropped. I didn't know where I'd landed, only that I'd better move on to a place where I felt secure, a place where I had friends.

In the morning, I woke with the sun and bathed in a sea translucent with early morning light. Then I headed for the mainland on the way back to New Orleans, looking forward to reconnecting with my friend Holly. This time I stayed in my car on the ferry crossing.

About the Author

Tamar Judith Rivers was born in Des Moines, Iowa, in 1946. She spent much of her childhood in Cincinnati, Ohio. Tamar spent the tumultuous late 1960s in San Francisco, and later moved to Austin, Texas, where she decided to stay. Tamar loved traveling around North America, visiting such places as New Mexico, Canada, Guatemala, Mexico, and the Omega Institute in Rhinebeck, New York.

Tamar was a peace and environmental activist, a massage therapist, yoga instructor, writer, singer, cook, fabulous potluck hostess, thrift store enthusiast, and animal lover (her dogs Bejeau and Allie, and her cat Goji held a special place in her heart). Tamar passed away in 2013, leaving behind two siblings, a niece, and many well-loved friends.